HOPE FOR CHRISTMAS

MALISSA CHAPIN

A Christmas Novella

Hope For Christmas

Malissa Chapin

Ivory Keys Press LLC

Hope For Christmas A Christmas Novella

Published by **Ivory Keys Press 2022 Oshkosh, Wisconsin**

ISBN 979-8-9851295-5-7 (Paperback)

ISBN 979-8-9851295-4-0 (Ebook)

Scripture quoted from the King James Version.

Cover Design by: Beck & Dot Book Covers

Editing by: Emerald Barnes

Contents

Chapter One

Merry Noel zipped her red Mustang into the parking space in front of the office building in downtown Atlanta. She hopped out, slammed the car door, and barked orders at her assistant into the phone as she hurried through the hall to catch an elevator. The old apartment building she'd tried to sell for the last six months finally had a buyer, and she couldn't afford to lose the sale. She needed to get rid of the property fast. With Christmas a week away and the holiday shutdown, she had no time to lose. The client had issued an ominous warning—if she didn't have the paperwork at the bank in an hour, they'd back out of the deal.

She stuck her hand into the closing elevator and pushed her way into the crowded space. The lady she forced aside frowned at Merry and rolled her eyes. "Excuse me, Miss Important," she whispered.

Merry whipped her head around and glared but continued barking orders into the phone. Throats cleared, and people shifted uncomfortably, but Merry ignored them. Merry had work to finish and money to make—no time for niceties. She stepped onto her floor, her bright red stilettos clicking on the tile as she hurried to her office. She calculated the commission she'd make on the sale and grinned—a perfect way to end the year—making money.

Laughter and loud Christmas music poured out of an office when a door opened. Merry scowled. "That better not be my office." She marched quicker and honed in on the door of Masters and Son's Realty while she walked. Laughter and music spilled out, filling the hallway when someone in a Santa hat walked into the hall.

Merry narrowed her eyes and sighed. *This is not good.* She had an hour to type the documents and send them to the client and no patience for an unannounced party in the office. She shoved the office door open and stared into the faces of her happy coworkers.

"Uh-oh," someone yelled in a back corner. "Ms. Scrooge is back. Quick, everyone, no more happiness." Laughter and hoots followed this comment, and someone tossed a piece of gold garland at Merry.

Merry paused, ready to defend herself but scowled and shook her head. She slammed the office door and sank into her chair. At least the door of her office muffled that cheesy Christmas music. Merry shuddered. Those popular Christmas songs set her teeth on edge, like when she accidentally drank sweet tea.

Merry grabbed a notepad and opened her laptop. She glanced at the clock—fifty-five minutes to earn several thousand dollars. She blew a breath to release some of the ever-present tension in her shoulders and typed furiously. She jabbed the button for her assistant, and Christmas music sounded loud and clear, filling her office with some nonsense about shoes. "Just hurry, please. I need you to run copies." Merry sighed and rubbed her forehead.

Her door opened, and Jayne scurried in, a huge green gift bow stuck in her hair and a plastic elf ears headband on her head.

Merry rolled her eyes. "Really, Jayne?"

Jayne shrugged. "What? It's Christmas, Merry, and I'm sorry, but I'd think you'd enjoy the season a little bit more with a name like yours." Jayne pouted and reached for the documents.

"My name is *Knoll*, Jayne—one syllable. Not no-el," Merry said.

Jayne shook her head. "I meant the Merry part. Your mother should have named you Sour." Jayne disappeared, leaving Merry alone in the dark office while holiday cheer leaked in the open door.

Merry jumped out of her chair to slam the door, but Oliver from accounting stepped in. He wore a fake Santa beard, and a red bulb ornament hung from his collar. "What do you need, Oliver?"

Oliver held up a plate of Christmas cookies and grinned. "Where did Jayne go? It's almost time for the gift exchange. Cookie?" He held the plate out to her, but she waved him away.

"She's working, Oliver. This is an office, not the North Pole."

Oliver frowned and said, "Good grief, Merry. No wonder they call you Scrooge. People like to have a little bit of cheer this time of year. Life is hard, Merry. Let people have their fun." He turned and marched away, and Merry kicked the door shut.

Merry Noel didn't participate in holiday cheer. She didn't eat Christmas cookies, listen to carols, or join the gift exchange. Like Oliver said, life might be challenging, but life also brought opportunities, and dancing through the office wearing Santa hats and dollar store ornaments didn't make anyone rich.

"Party on the weekend if you need a break from your miserable life," she said.

"What's that?" Jayne set the papers on the desk. "You're lucky. That stupid printer kept jamming, but I managed. Are you driving them to the bank?" Jayne glanced at the clock.

"Yes, but I need you to scan this pile into the computer." Merry pointed at a tall stack of documents on the corner of her desk.

Jayne's smile faded. "But, Merry, it's ..." she pointed behind her to the party. A crash and raucous laughter poured through the open door.

Merry narrowed her eyes. "Seriously, Jayne? No one told me there was a party today, or I'd have made different arrangements for this sale."

"Do you know why no one tells you there's a party, Merry? No one likes you, that's why. Because we can't stand how ugly you are about our fun. You make rude comments, roll your eyes, and insult everyone. We like to hang out together, and one afternoon a year to celebrate Christmas isn't too much to ask. We have permission to hold the party in the office today, and I don't need your approval. Scan them yourself." Jayne bounced out of Merry's office.

She returned a moment later and said, "And I have no idea why I care, Merry Noel, but if the happiness of others hurts you so much, you need to get help. Something is seriously wrong with you. You're a Scrooge, and you deserve all the misery you get."

Merry watched as Jayne's shadow march away.

When did Jayne grow a backbone?

Jayne's accusations stung and rang in her mind. *"Because no one likes you, Merry."*

Merry lifted her chin and grabbed the stack of documents and her purse. She gulped a slurp of cold coffee from the mug on her desk and opened her office door. Every eye in the room turned and stared.

"I don't really care if you people don't like me." She raised her eyebrows and shouted. "I don't like you either. You are the laziest co-workers I've ever seen, and if I were the boss, I'd fire every one of you." She knocked the folders off the corner of Oliver's desk and every desk along the aisle. She dumped a platter of cookies on the floor and yanked the wreath off the office door. A few people snickered, but the others turned away.

"Turn up the music" someone shouted.

Merry marched to the door with her head held high. Cheerful music rang in her ears all the way to the elevator, and her nerves shook with every note.

Chapter Two

Merry nosed her Mustang into traffic and took several deep breaths to calm her nerves. *"Because no one likes you, Merry,"* echoed. She gritted her teeth at the traffic moving impossibly slow. When her phone rang, she grabbed it, expecting Jayne to pour out a heartfelt apology, but she had no time for sentiment or feelings.

"What?" Merry barked into the phone.

"My goodness, Merry Noel." Her mother's voice oozed hurt. "What's gotten into you? It's Christmas."

"I didn't know it was you, for one thing, Mother," Merry said, her tone softer—a little.

"And I'm in the middle of traffic on a time crunch right now."

Her mother sighed. "I don't know how you do it, honey. I'd never handle all that traffic and noise. I'll let you go. I just wondered what day are you getting here?"

"What?"

"What day are you arriving home?" her mother repeated slowly, emphasizing every word.

Merry blew out a breath. "Mom, I'm not coming home. What gave you that idea? I am up to my eyeballs in paperwork and closings and don't have time for a little jaunt to Wisconsin." She laughed. "You sure you're okay?"

"Merry, when we talked in October, you said 'sure' when I asked if you were coming home. I have everything ready. All your favorites ..." she trailed off, disappointment oozing through the phone, loud and clear.

"So, from a flippant comment I made in October, you assumed I'd drop everything and run up there for a holiday I despise?" Merry laughed.

"Well, you didn't always hate Christmas, Merry. And I ... well, I need you, Merry Noel." Mother's voice dropped to a whisper, and Merry heard the little hitch that promised tears in 3 ... 2 ... 1 ...

"Sorry for the misunderstanding, Mom. I'm definitely not coming home. Gotta go." She clicked off the call and tossed her phone into the passenger seat. She slammed on her brakes as the truck in front of her stopped. She glanced at the car clock and groaned. Three miles to go in bumper-to-bumper traffic and only ten minutes of that hour left.

She gripped the steering wheel and debated whether or not to call her client. If she tipped him off that she was running late, he'd balk for sure.

She tapped the steering wheel with her finger and shook her head. Her mother was hilarious. *Me? Coming home for Christmas? She's crazy.*

Merry circled the parking ramp for the third time and found a spot on the top floor. She set the parking brake and ran to the elevator. Already ten minutes late, she had no time to lose. Her heels tapped on the cement floor, and her blood pressure skyrocketed. Every second took money from her bonus, and she needed every penny to pay for her designer condo. Merry grabbed the tiny Post-It note taped to the center of the doors. “Elevator out of order? No!” Merry banged on the doors and gritted her teeth.

She whirled around and hurried to the staircase door, clutching her briefcase and purse. The stilettoes pinched her toes, and her head pounded. She was late—too late—but she had to show up. Her reputation was on the line, and she didn't need this banker telling clients that she missed appointments.

She ran toward the bank, huffing and puffing. Her hair had worked its way loose from the bun, and she hadn't applied fresh lipstick. Her blouse stuck to her underarms, and the damp cloth worried her.

Please don't let me smell.

Merry needed this sale to go through, and she wanted that bonus. The busyness of her job and the fast-paced schedule helped her cope with life—no time to mope. Making money helped her self-esteem, and she needed a dose of that right now because she knew this appointment would be abysmal. She shoved into the bank doors and sped up, but she didn't stop to glance around the lobby before she barreled through the space.

The next thing Merry heard was, "Are you okay ma'am? Oh my goodness, I'm so sorry." A gentle voice reached her ears, but her mind couldn't comprehend why she was staring at the ceiling.

Merry opened her eyes and stared into the face of a worried woman. The woman held out her hand, but Merry ignored her and glanced around.

She frowned. “What in the world just happened?”

The woman grimaced. “I’m so sorry. You ran through the doors and tripped on our stroller.” She pointed to a contraption holding a toddler.

Merry raised her eyebrows at the crumbs smeared across the child’s face. The baby grinned and waved a cracker at Merry. She turned away from the dirty-faced gremlin and stared at the woman who held out her hand.

“Let me help you up,” the woman said. “Can I get you anything?”

Merry glanced at her shoe lying next to her—minus one stiletto heel—and rolled her eyes. “No. I believe you’ve done enough.”

The woman’s eyes flooded with tears. “I’m really sorry, Miss. I’d never hurt anyone. I just ... you ran through the door ... you ...” She grabbed the stroller and wheeled through the door, leaving Merry sitting on the floor in the middle of a busy bank.

She blew out her breath, grabbed her broken shoe and her briefcase, and unfolded from the floor. She held her shoe and stared for a moment. Limping across the rest of the lobby on one stiletto and one broken heel didn't seem like the best way to make a good impression.

Merry snapped the heel off her other shoe and slipped it on her foot. She lifted her chin and pretended she hadn't just ruined an expensive pair of shoes and humiliated herself in the worst way imaginable. She didn't have time to feel sorry for herself, so she squared her shoulders and marched to the office of the loan manager. She didn't glance at the clock, and she didn't make excuses. She smoothed her hair and pasted on a smile.

"John Worthington, please," she said to the receptionist.

The receptionist raised an eyebrow and pushed a button on the desk. She spoke into the phone and pointed to a door across the room.

Merry marched across the room on her broken heels with her head held high until she caught a glimpse of herself in a mirror.

Her hair stood out from her head in a Medusa-like fashion. Pink lipstick smeared across one cheek, and mascara dripped down the other one.

Oh no. I must have wiped my face when I tried to sit up. Too late now.

The office door opened. "Merry?" The loan officer she had worked with stood in the doorway, scowling. "You're late. Your client left half an hour ago. What happened?"

Merry clenched her jaw and inhaled.

I will not cry. I will not cry.

"I'm sorry, Mr. Worthington. Traffic."

Worthington raised his eyebrows and shrugged his shoulders. "I'm sorry, but he's gone. He said to let you know the deal is off and do not call him."

Merry nodded and turned to leave.

"I'm sorry, Merry," he called. "Have a good Christmas."

Merry waved her hand and shook her head.

Merry Christmas. Bah Humbug.

Chapter Three

Merry limped to the parking garage on the broken heels. Passersby stared, but she lifted her chin and glared, her eyes shooting darts. A woman dressed in an ugly Christmas sweater stood at the corner, ringing a bell. She opened her mouth when Merry passed but shut it again at Merry's fierce stare.

A department store on the block piped Christmas music onto the street, the notes plucking Merry's last nerve. A mother pulled her children close when Merry stormed past, and for the first time in hours, Merry smiled.

Yes, keep your dirty kids away from me.

Merry limped up the stairs to her car. She would hop in, drive home, and forget about this terrible, horrible day. A bubble bath and a good book might do the trick—that and the pound of chocolates her boss had given her for Christmas. She hobbled across the garage and breathed a sigh of relief when she reached her Mustang.

Just a few more steps and I can put this miserable day behind me.

She rounded the corner and dropped her briefcase. "A flat tire? Are you kidding me?" she yelled. Her angry voice echoed around the garage, and she widened her eyes to stop the tears that pressed the back of her eyes. Merry punched in the number of a towing service and plopped into the driver's seat to wait for rescue.

She closed her eyes and replayed the day. No sale. No bonus. No dignity. No tire. An unhappy mother. Throbbing feet. Misery.

Merry rubbed her eyes and sighed. The office was closed for the next several days, so she'd hole up in her condo and get her blood pressure back in order. The lost sale hurt, but she'd get over it. There was always another sale.

An hour later, she was on her way home on a fresh tire. The traffic crawled, and her frazzled nerves shook. "Why do I live here? I hate this traffic." On a typical day, she listened to a podcast or audiobook, and the traffic didn't faze her. But today, she hated big city life.

"You can always come home," her mother's voice whispered.

"No, Mom, I'm not coming home," she said.

Visions of home tumbled in her head—an old house, a dilapidated red barn, a tiny town, backward people acting as if their little lives mattered. Her retired nurse mother took care of every stray and down-on-their-luck person in town. Merry shuddered.

Not falling for that trap, Mother.

Merry pulled into her parking spot and tromped to the entrance of her building. The doorman raised his eyebrow when he held the door open. She shook her head, and he nodded. Merry sighed and pulled her bag onto her shoulders. Her feet and calves stung, and her hair flew around her face, but she didn't care. All she wanted was to shut her door behind her and drown her sorrows in chocolate and a book—maybe she'd binge-watch her favorite series.

She wobbled off the elevator and whispered a prayer. "Please don't let Mrs. Cromby see me. That's all I'm asking for the entire season. Okay?"

She grabbed her keys and glanced down the hall. Empty. She breathed a sigh of relief and quickened her steps. Home free.

Merry was one door away from her condo when the door opened, and Mrs. Cromby stepped into the hall dressed head to toe in Christmas tacky. Merry blew out an impatient sigh.

Mrs. Cromby held out a plate of cookies. "Bless your heart. You look a sight. Cookies?

Did you have a bad day? What happened? Want to talk?"

Merry shook her head and winced at the pain in her heel. "No, everything's fine, Mrs. Cromby."

"Well, I don't believe that for a second, but if you insist." The woman raised her eyebrows and rested a hand on her hip. "Where are you going for Christmas dinner? Have you invited anyone over? I hate to think of you all alone. Where's your family? Why don't you come to our party on Christmas Eve?"

Merry sighed. "Thank you, but no. I'm not in the mood for your cheesy Christmas party."

Mrs. Cromby frowned and said, "Well, excuse me, Merry Noel."

Merry narrowed her eyes and said, "It's pronounced *knoll*, Mrs. Cromby. Not No-el."

"No need to be rude, Merry," Mrs. Cromby said.

Christmas music floated down the hall. Merry hurried into her condo and shut her door to drown out the awful sound. She smiled and glanced around—zero evidence of Christmas.

The stark black and white décor and the view of the city refreshed Merry. She sighed, kicked off her broken shoes, and sank onto the couch, allowing the silence to soak into her soul. Merry took a deep breath and pushed her exhausted body off the couch.

"First things first," she said and grabbed her broken shoes, tossing them in the trash. She shook her head and said, "I loved those shoes." She padded to the refrigerator and peeked inside. "Empty," Merry groaned. She had forgotten to stop for groceries on the way home.

She brewed a cup of coffee and ran through the list of her favorite take-out restaurants but couldn't decide what to eat. She sighed and flipped through the channels on the television. "Christmas. Christmas concert. Syrupy-sweet-make-me-gag romance," she said while flipping through channels. "What did I expect on a Friday night three days before Christmas?" She tossed the remote on the cushion and rested her throbbing feet on the coffee table. Merry gazed out the window at the city but didn't smile this time.

Her designer condo with a fantastic view of downtown Atlanta usually filled her with pride and contentment. She had attained her dream of living and working in the big city and affording luxuries. She was too busy to socialize. Too busy for church. Too busy for friends. Mrs. Cromby across the hall was the closest acquaintance Merry had, and she avoided Mrs. Cromby like the plague.

Merry sighed and whispered, "It's just Christmas that has me down. These fake movies are trying to fill me with sadness because my life isn't their ideal. I'm not falling for it. Who needs snow and romance to have a good life? I certainly don't."

Merry clicked off the television and ran a hot bath. Perhaps a bubble bath and her book would settle her churning mind.

Chapter Four

Merry toweled off and hummed a tune—not a Christmas tune—but a song nonetheless. The steamy tub full of bubbles had worked a miracle. Halfway through her soak, she had decided to order Chinese food. She'd eat while watching the shows on her DVR, then read until she fell asleep.

Merry pulled on her fluffiest sweats and dried her hair. She grabbed her phone to order dinner and frowned at the notification on her screen. "Why is the boss calling me on a Friday night?" She thought through the day, wondering if she had forgotten something important. *Maybe he needs me to work over the weekend.* Merry dialed the boss's number while scrolling through the restaurant's menu, deciding between egg rolls and lo mein.

"Merry," her boss said. "I'm sorry I didn't catch you in the office today."

"No problem," Merry said. "Did you need me to work this weekend? I don't have any pressing plans." Merry frowned at the silence on the other end of the line. "Hello? If you need me to cover for someone, I don't mind."

Her boss cleared his throat and said, "Well, I ... well, it's ... I'm sorry to do this by phone, Merry, but here's the deal. We are letting you go."

Merry stared at the phone and shook her head. "Wait. It sounded like you said you were letting me go. Go? Where? A new office?"

"No, Merry. The company restructured several positions, and your position moved to another department."

"That's fine. Where is the office?" she asked.

He cleared his throat again. "That's the reason I called, Merry. You aren't moving. Your job is gone."

"Wait a minute! What? I have more seniority than half that office. What do you mean my job is gone?" She jumped from the couch and ran her fingers through her hair. Merry glanced around her impeccably decorated condo and shook her head. "Why?"

"The missed opportunity this afternoon and several complaints about your drain on the atmosphere in the office settled our decision. I had nothing to do with this, Merry. You do good work."

"My drain on the atmosphere in the office?" She spat each word through gritted teeth, barely holding her rage in check. Exploding on the poor man wouldn't help her case. "I'll change. I need this job, please." Merry hated the way her voice made her sound like a beggar.

"What was the knocking things off desks and yelling about?"

Merry sighed.

"Well, as I said, Merry, I'm sorry, but the decision was out of my hands. There's a severance package, of course. HR will mail your paperwork and the details. I'm sorry to ruin your Christmas." The call ended, and Merry dropped onto her couch.

"You cannot ruin something I won't celebrate," she whispered. "The atmosphere in the office? Are you kidding me?" Merry punched a black and white chevron pillow and jumped up from the sofa. She paced the living room—her expensive living room.

"What am I going to do? I can't afford to live here without a job." Merry walked to the window and gazed at the city. Lights twinkled, and traffic snaked along the road below. She loved this view most of the time, but the scene blinked dollar signs tonight. She blew out a deep breath and gave herself a pep talk. "I can get another job. Relax." She mentally ran her budget numbers and sighed. "It's gonna take a miracle to keep me in this condo." She groaned.

A thought flitted through her worries, and she shook her head and frowned.

"You can always come home, Merry," her mom had said. Merry sighed, remembering how rude she'd been to her mother earlier that

afternoon—back when she had an important job and lots of money.

"Mom, you don't want me there ruining your holiday with my lack of Christmas spirit," Merry whispered and leaned against the plate glass window. She watched the traffic for several more minutes, then pushed away from the window, hurrying to her room. Merry stuffed clothes and a toothbrush into a bag and ran around the condo, unplugging appliances. She flipped off the lights and grabbed the box by the door—her mom's Christmas gift she'd forgotten to mail.

Merry stepped into the hallway and carefully inched her door closed with a quiet click. She held her breath and slowly turned the key in the lock to avoid making a sound. She turned from her door with a sigh. *I made it without alerting Mrs. Big Nose.* A smile spread across Merry's face, and she turned into the stare of her neighbor. Mrs. Cromby stood in the middle of the hallway, wiping her hands on a poinsettia dish towel. Bing Crosby's crooning voice spilled into the space—Merry's least favorite Christmas singer.

"Going somewhere, Merry?" Mrs. Cromby asked. "Are you sure you won't come over for cookies?"

"Gotta run, sorry."

Mrs. Cromby's shrill laugh echoed down the hall, and she called, "Where are you off to in such a hurry? I'll convince you to stop in one of these days."

Merry waved and hurried down the hall, whispering, "One of these days, I'll sneak out of my condo without you noticing."

She stepped into the elevator and sighed. Mrs. Cromby's meddling shredded her last nerve, and her left eye twitched. She leaned her head back and counted the ding of the bell as the elevator passed each floor. "What an absolutely ridiculous day," she whispered to herself and laughed a mirthless laugh as she hurried to the parking garage.

Chapter Five

Merry settled into the driver's seat, entered 1225 Noel Lane in her maps app, and sighed—thirteen hours if everything went well. "I can do this," she whispered and cranked up the radio. Merry drove through the night, changing the radio station whenever a Christmas tune played.

Merry exited the highway somewhere outside of Nashville and parked at a truck stop. She needed caffeine and snacks. When she sat her selection on the counter, a middle-aged woman with blonde hair piled high stepped to the cash register and smiled. "Hey, sugar. You headin' home for Christmas?"

Merry's eyes widened, and she stared at the woman for a moment, unable to speak as sudden tears pressed the back of her eyes. She nodded and dug in her purse for cash.

"Hey, sweetie," the woman said, leaning across the counter to touch Merry's hand. "I don't know what you're facing or what's causing those tears, but you remember this. You can do this. You can go home and face whatever's hurtin' ya. You are strong, and you are loved. You need a hug?"

Merry glanced at the hand touching her arm and nodded. Merry wasn't a hugger—even had a T-shirt announcing that fact. But something about this woman's kindness broke down Merry's defenses, and she *did* want a hug from the stranger.

The woman hurried around the counter, pulled Merry close, and squeezed. The woman patted Merry's back and whispered, "You go home and have a good time with your loved ones, baby. You're going home for something important. Someone needs ya—I can feel it."

"For crying out loud, Trixie, I need to pay for my fuel and get back on the road," a voice hollered from the line of customers that had accumulated since Trixie left her post to hug Merry.

"Stuff it, Chris. This little chickadee needed a hug, and it's Christmas," the woman hollered. She smiled at Merry. "Name's Trixie, sugar. What's yours?"

Merry sniffled a tiny sniffle and wiped her damp eyes. "Merry."

"Well, ain't that the best name for this time of year. Your coffee is on me tonight, darlin'. You drive safe and get home and love on your people. Where you headed?"

The man from the back of the line cleared his throat in a loud, exaggerated rumble, and Trixie glared at him and shook her head.

"Wisconsin," Merry whispered.

"Oh, goodness, baby. I hope you grabbed your coat. I heard they have lots of snow on the way."

Merry smiled and shrugged. "Well, that's normal. Thank you for the coffee and ..."

Trixie waved her hand. “It’s nothing, sugar. Now, you get home safe and remember what Trixie told ya. There’s a reason you’re on your way now. I just know it.”

Merry smiled, grabbed her snacks and coffee, and hurried past the trucker who glanced at his watch, frowning.

“Good grief, Chris, you aren’t in that much of a hurry,” Trixie winked at Merry. “Bye, sweetheart.”

Merry waved and hurried to her car, replaying the cashier’s words. ”*You’re on your way home for a reason.*”

“If you must know, Trixie,” she muttered to herself. “I lost my job, and I’m about to go broke. That’s the reason.” Merry sighed and pulled onto the highway. Her wheels pointing toward home.

The sun rose as Merry drove past the “Welcome to Wisconsin” sign. She smiled, remembering all the family vacations they had taken. Dad said he loved that sign because it meant they were almost home. Merry had made a game of trying to see the sign before anyone else. She'd shout, "Almost home," and Dad would shake his head and smile.

"Almost home," she whispered. "I win, Daddy." Tears stung her eyes, and she shook them away—no time for melting down.

Merry gripped the wheel and saluted the cheese castle. "Haven't seen a cheese castle lately." She smiled. Wisconsin loved cheese—and the Packers—and Merry didn't. "Probably half the reason I moved away," she said.

She glanced at the maps app, ninety miles to Liberty Ridge—home. "And no fresh snow, Trixie," she said, remembering the kind stranger at the truck stop. Merry preferred no snow. She'd grown accustomed to brown Christmases and dry roads for winter driving. Living in the south had spoiled Merry and left her shivering with any blast of air below fifty degrees.

Merry adjusted the heat knob and blew the vent in her direction. "And I'm not even out of the car." She sighed. "It's gonna be a long couple of days."

When Merry's car crested the hill, Liberty Ridge lay before her, nestled in a valley surrounded by rolling hills. Her heart squeezed at the sight of the small town, but Merry didn't know if the squeeze was happiness or regret. She sighed and tapped her brakes to slow down as she entered the small town. She didn't need a welcome home speeding ticket.

Chapter Six

Merry drove through Liberty Ridge, her heart pounding. *What a stupid idea. What was I thinking?* She gripped the wheel and considered pulling back onto the highway and driving straight back to Atlanta. Until she drove down Main Street, she hadn't thought about what coming home meant. All the well-meaning people. All the questions. All the things Merry didn't want to talk about. All the reasons she had left this little town behind.

Merry sighed at the Christmas baubles decorating every square inch of the town. Candy canes hung from the light poles, lights hung from every awning, and wreaths hung on every door. Merry's ears hurt from the Christmas music and jingle bells ringing through her rolled-up car windows. A large sleigh parked in the downtown greenspace held a mechanical Santa waving and yelling, "Ho, ho, ho ..."

Two large horses harnessed to a wagon sat next to city hall, and a group of people dressed in Dickens-era costumes walked down the sidewalk ahead of her. Merry shook her head. "It's seven in the morning, people. What in the world?"

Merry nosed her Mustang into a parking space in front of the café. A bright sign hung over the door, "Peppermint Patty's Snack Bar." Merry glanced down the street at the other shops. They all sported shiny temporary signs painted red and green. When Merry read "Mistletoe Music Store" and "Bailey Bros. Building and Loan," she groaned. "Over the top," she whispered.

Merry pulled open the door to the Peppermint Patty's Snack Bar. Bells jingled overhead, and Perry Como's voice crooned some carol or another. The café bustled with customers and servers, but Merry found a seat in the corner near the window. She slid into the booth and grabbed a menu. She needed to fortify herself with eggs and coffee before she went home, but she second-guessed her decision to stop for breakfast as she gazed at all of the Christmas fripperies.

A waitress wearing elf ears stepped to the table. "Morning, what can I get you?" She glanced up from her notepad. "Merry? Merry Noel? What are you doing here? Your mama said you couldn't make it home this year."

"You work here, Patty?" Merry asked.

"Own the place. I bought it a few years ago after Arnold retired. I guess it was right after your ..." Patty stopped, and her eyes widened. She patted Merry's shoulder. "What can I get you?"

Merry ordered an omelet and coffee and attempted a weak smile, thankful that Patty hadn't pressed the issue.

"Coming right up. Are you taking your mom to the Jingle Mingle?" Patty asked. Her cheerful smile and sparkling eyes clouded when Merry shook her head. "Well ..." Patty turned away and hurried to the kitchen, leaving Merry to deal with guilt for apparently ruining Patty's morning. A troop of ballerinas in puffy tulle tutus ran past the window. The girls' smiles reminded Merry of the year she was the Sugarplum Fairy for the Jingle Mingle.

How did I forget Jingle Mingle? Liberty Ridge's annual festival, the last weekend before Christmas, explained the false signs and nostalgic Christmas decorations around the town square. Merry groaned at her continued lousy luck. *Of all the weekends to finally decide to come home, I pick the Jingle Mingle.*

Merry held the warm mug of coffee decorated with holly and berries and stared out the window at the activity in the park to avoid the questioning eyes in the café. Too many of them knew her family. They'd have questions she didn't care to answer, or they'd say something that would make her resolve to visit mother crumble. She'd eat her eggs and drink her coffee, then head down the road to Noel Lane and face her mom.

I should have stopped at the gas station for a greasy sandwich. Merry sighed and sipped the coffee, wondering what had possessed her to come home. She'd avoided home for so long, and now she was stuck in a Christmas nightmare.

Merry paid her bill and slipped out before Patty could ask any more questions. She braced herself before stepping onto the sidewalk. She had forgotten how to walk on ice and snow, and the last thing she needed was to wipe out on the sidewalk on Main Street. The entire town would laugh at her expense and make fun of her for being too southern. She remembered falling at the bank yesterday—no ice in sight. She imagined how ridiculous she looked with her body splayed on the floor and groaned.

Merry walked gingerly to the car, dreaming of warmth and ice-free sidewalks.

She reached for her car door and screamed when a man in full wise man costume stood up from the front of her car. "What are you doing?" she asked as she stepped to the front of her Mustang. A wreath hung from the grill of her car, and her eyes widened. "Why is that on my car?" Pressure rose in her chest, and she bit her tongue because she was about to spill every ounce of her pent-up frustration on this stranger.

He stood in front of her car with a deer in the headlights look. "I'm supposed to attach a wreath to every car on Main Street today. It's a gift from the chamber of commerce." He smiled a lopsided smile that may have endeared Merry to the man in the past, but today, the smile fried her last nerve.

Merry clenched her fists, "Get that off my car right now."

The man adjusted his crown and hurried to the grill, pulling the wreath off of her car. "I'm sorry, ma'am. I didn't mean to upset you. My apologies. Really." He backed away, stammering as if Merry had pulled a weapon on him.

She dropped into her car and slammed it into gear, narrowly avoiding a group of choir boys running across the street—time to get this miserable visit over.

Chapter Seven

Merry pulled into traffic, watching for costumed pedestrians. She tapped the brakes for a nutcracker, an elf, and a shepherd leading a camel and four sheep. She sighed and pasted on a fake smile as the pedestrians waved and yelled, "Merry Christmas." *Why oh why did you forget the Jingle Mingle, Merry?* She nodded at a straggling shepherd as she moved past the crowd and pointed her car toward 1225 Noel Lane.

Merry's great-grandfather, John Noel, had purchased the land a hundred years ago, and keeping it in the family was a massive point of pride for the Noels. When Marquette County named roads in the middle of the last century, her grandfather had insisted the road's name was Noel Lane after their family. Grandpa may have greased the palm of a county official or two, but no one mentioned that.

Merry hadn't minded living in the country when she was young. The farm had plenty of room to roam, and she had played and hid in every nook and cranny of their land. The bright red barn had been her favorite place to escape with a book. Daddy would find her curled up in the hay in an empty stall and tell her to hurry in for supper.

Merry smiled, and a pang of regret twisted her heart. *When did I start hating the farm?*

She couldn't pinpoint an exact moment but imagined her teen years had changed her mind. When she missed too many activities because of farm work or when her newest crush turned up his nose and said, "You don't shovel manure, do you?" The charm of the family homestead had withered somewhere in there, and Merry dreamed dreams of city life, clean work, and nights of full sleep uninterrupted by a birthing cow.

Her parents had never scolded her for her dreams or asked her to stay on the farm. They supported her—silly dreams and all. She had left her parents and the farm far behind while she created the life she had dreamed of. She decorated her downtown Atlanta condo in an impeccable modern style but rarely spent time there and never hosted guests. Her busy job left no time for visits home. Merry Noel was too busy and too important to drop everything and come back to Wisconsin to visit family. But somewhere along the way, Merry Noel had lost her community; friendships faded; and soon, very important, very busy Merry Noel found herself drifting friendless in the big city—well, except for Mrs. Cromby, who never left Merry alone.

Merry sighed. *What is it about this place that makes me reflective? I'm perfectly happy in Atlanta.* She turned onto Noel Lane, and the homestead lay before her. The red barn covered in snow dripped icicles from the eaves.

Her mom had hung pine garlands and wreaths on the barn. The wreaths hanging on every window of the white farmhouse took her breath away, and a lump rose in her throat.

"Coming home shouldn't hurt this much," she whispered and widened her eyes to banish the tears stinging her eyes. "I'm just tired after driving all night," she whispered. "Yes, that's all."

Merry parked the Mustang in the spot behind the barn and grabbed her bag from the trunk. Snow crunched under her feet as she hurried up the path to the back door. The snow glittered in the sun, and Merry remembered when she used to believe every glittering snowflake was a diamond. She smiled at the snowbank rising next to the path.

"We'd all be rich," she whispered.

The back door was unlocked—as always. Merry pushed the door open and called, "Mom?" She dropped the bag on the table and left her shoes on a mat near the back door. Mom didn't allow shoes in the house, and she wasn't about to start this visit with mom correcting her for breaking the rules.

"Mom," she called louder as she moved through the house. "Hmmm."

The quiet house was chilly, and Merry pulled her sweater tight. She moved to the woodstove and added logs. The wood crackled, and the flame danced as Merry inhaled. She had forgotten the fragrance of a wood fire.

She stood and glanced around the room. "I've forgotten a lot, apparently. Like the fact that my mother is most likely at the Jingle Mingle," Merry sighed and plopped on the worn sofa—the same one they bought when she was ten. The cushions hugged her, and Merry curled up in the corner, pulling the multi-colored crocheted afghan over her as she drifted to sleep.

The back door banged open, and Merry jumped. Her heart pounded as she rubbed grit from her eyes. She focused on a shadow moving through the kitchen. The footsteps were far too heavy to be her mother's. Merry glanced around for the shotgun Daddy had always leaned in the corner in case a predator attacked the chickens. She tiptoed to the corner behind the recliner and grabbed the gun—no time to check for bullets, but the intruder would never know.

She tiptoed to the kitchen and leveled the gun at the costumed person searching her mother's cupboards. "What are you doing?" she demanded, and the person whirled around, dropping a plate that smashed to the floor. "You?" Merry said to the wise man she'd chased away from her Mustang earlier. "What are you doing here?"

The wise man held up his hands and stared at her with wide eyes. "Put that thing down."

"Not until you tell me why you're going through the cupboards," Merry said.

The wise man crossed his arms and peered down his nose. "I should ask you the same thing. What are *you* doing in Ivy's house? Hmm?"

"I asked first," she said and held the shotgun level.

The wise man pointed to the floor and shrugged. "Miss Ivy forgot her fruitcake for the competition, and I offered to run out here for her and grab it. But you scared me, and I dropped it."

Merry glanced at the pile of glass shards and pieces of fruitcake on the floor and groaned.

"She's not going to be very happy," the wise man said.

"Yeah? Well, she's not going to be very happy to see your big clodhopper footprints on her kitchen floor either. You can't know her very well if you didn't take your shoes off," Merry said.

"Well, excuse me," the wise man said. His crown slipped onto his forehead, and Merry held back a smirk. "Put the gun down for crying out loud," he said. "I'm Joe, and I help Ivy out around here now and then."

Merry lowered the gun and stared. "A wise man named Joe, huh? Sounds about right for this crazy town. You get going and figure out what you're going to tell her, and I'll clean up this mess."

Wise Man Joe leaned on the counter; his arms crossed. "Not so fast, Gunshot Sue. Who are you?"

Merry looked up from grabbing pieces of glass from the floor and said, "I'm Ivy's daughter, Merry."

The man's eyes widened, and a broad grin spread over his face. "Wait 'til she hears ..."

"Please don't. Don't tell her I'm home," Merry begged.

Wise Man Joe frowned. "Okay, my lips are sealed, but she'll love the surprise. Ivy has told me all about you."

Merry rolled her eyes. "Oh, I'm sure she has. Now get out of here so I can clean this disaster before she sees what you did."

"Should I take one of her plates and grab a fruitcake at the grocery store?" the man asked.

Merry's eyes bugged out, and she stood from the floor, her hands on her hips. "If you think my mother would enter a store-bought fruitcake in a competition, you're not very wise, Wise Man Joe." Merry blew out a breath. "You're better off telling her you ran over her favorite chicken than to sabotage her entry. Ivy Noel has won the Jingle Mingle fruitcake baking competition for the last twenty years, and she didn't win the contest with store-bought fruitcake."

"Twenty-five," Wise Man Joe said. "She's won the competition the last twenty-five years. I'm in trouble, huh?"

Merry grimaced and shrugged. "Not sure what to tell ya there, wise guy, but you're gonna face worse trouble if you don't get your dripping shoes off of Ivy Noel's kitchen floor."

Wise Man Joe nodded and slipped out the back door, leaving Merry to remove the evidence.

Chapter Eight

Merry swept away the remains of her mother's prize-winning fruitcake and wiped the floor. She cleaned Wise Man Joe's path of footprints and glanced around the kitchen as childhood memories flooded her. *Why did I come?*

Merry dug through the cupboards for coffee and brewed a large pot. She poured the hot liquid into a jumbo Christmas mug and settled into the corner of the sofa, gathering the afghan around her. The lights on the Christmas tree twinkled, and Merry glanced around the living room.

How can everything be the same and yet so completely different? Her mother's decorating style was not farmhouse chic or modern—just farmhouse. When teenage Merry had complained that they didn't have anything matching anywhere in the entire house, her mom had smiled and shrugged. "We live on a working farm, Merry. Dirt and animal things get tracked in. Half the time, there's a baby animal or two in my kitchen. I'd yell at anyone who got things dirty if I had nice furniture. This way, I can enjoy my life and not worry about furniture."

"But you do care about your clean kitchen floor, Mom." Merry smiled and glanced at the clock. The festival would last for at least two more hours. She sunk into the couch, put her head back, and dozed.

A strong arm lifted her, and Merry felt the stubble on her daddy's chin. She rested her cheek against the rough wool of his coat. "Time for you to go to bed, my sweet Merry Bell," he whispered against her hair. Merry snuggled down into his arms and let him carry her to bed. He tucked her in and pulled the covers to her chin. He smoothed her hair and kissed her forehead. "Sweet dreams."

Merry sat up and swallowed over the lump in her throat. "Daddy?" she whispered and glanced around. "I felt him," she said. She walked across the room to the woodstove where three stockings hung. "Why three, Mom?" Merry sighed. Photos in silver frames lined the shelf next to the stove. Merry grabbed one and stared at her father. He wore his best suit and his brilliant smile. Merry rubbed her finger across his face, and a tear rolled down her cheek.

She leaned the frame on the shelf and swallowed over the lump in her throat. She turned away from the photos. "Unbelievable," she whispered.

The kitchen door opened. "Merry? Merry Noel? Are you here?" her mother called from the kitchen. Merry wiped her eyes and gulped a deep breath.

"In here, Mom," she called.

Ivy Noel came around the corner, pulled off her gloves, and laughed. “You said you weren’t coming!”

Merry shrugged. “Changed my mind.” No need to explain the lost job and the lost sale.

“Well, come here, and hug your mother. I’m so glad you came home.” She pulled Merry into a tight hug and patted her back. “How long can you stay?”

“A few days, Mom. I’m not sure.”

Ivy nodded and smiled. “Good. Then you’ll be home for Christmas.”

Visions of parties, Christmas music, and mirth flitted through her head at the phrase “home for Christmas.” She sighed. *I can’t do this.*

“Sorry about your fruitcake, Mom,” Merry said. She sat at the kitchen table wrapped in the couch afghan, sipping hot cocoa.

Ivy shrugged and said, “Well, that’s my fault for letting Joe come get it. I should have known better." She smiled. "Can't win them all, I guess. And Flossie Wright almost passed out from excitement when she won. I enjoyed seeing her happiness. Winning the contest made her entire Christmas."

Merry watched her mom wipe the clean countertops and organize the meticulously organized cupboards. Her mom had always been fastidious—nothing had changed. "Do you need me to help, Mom?"

Ivy stopped scrubbing the clean counter and glanced out the window. "Do you remember how to feed the chickens?"

Merry frowned. "Of course I do, Mom. I haven't been gone that long. Two scoops?"

Her mom nodded and said, "The scoop is hanging inside the door. Thank you, sweetie."

Merry tugged on the boots at the backdoor and slipped into her jacket. The gray sky and crisp air reminded Merry of every childhood Christmas. She inhaled the clean air and sighed. She hated to admit that the atmosphere here was far better than the polluted air in downtown Atlanta. She couldn't remember the last time she'd taken a deep breath of city air.

The chickens clucked when she opened the door of their coop. She smiled and called their names. Yesterday, she worked in a busy office, earning a hefty salary, and today, she was unemployed feeding her mother's chickens. "What a life," she whispered to the chickens. She scooped their grain, refilled water, and trudged through the snow back to the house.

Merry stopped halfway to the house and turned in a slow circle, taking in her childhood home. The paint on the red barn wasn't as bright as she remembered, but it still had a cheerful Christmasy sort of appearance. Smoke curled from the farmhouse chimney, and the scent of hardwood smoke drifted down to Merry's nose. The air smelled like a woodstove, and Merry sniffed again—snow.

"Hey, Mom, did the weather report mention snow?" Merry asked as she unbundled in the kitchen.

"I believe I heard something about it, but I didn't pay attention." Ivy stirred milk on the stove. "More cocoa?"

"Sure." Merry smiled and sank onto the kitchen chair. Her mom poured hot chocolate into a mug, dropped a peppermint candy into the bottom, and dolloped whipped cream on top. She handed the steaming mug to Merry.

Ivy sat in the chair across from Merry and smiled. "Why are you home? Really?" Her eyes flooded with concern as she stared at Merry with her mom look.

Merry shrugged. "Do I need a reason to come home, Mom?"

"Never. But yesterday afternoon, you told me in no uncertain terms that you weren't coming home and that you didn't celebrate Christmas. Then you show up after obviously driving all night. Makes a mother wonder what's going on. That's all." Ivy stood up and patted Merry's back on her way to the sink to wash the cocoa pan.

"Christmas Eve is tomorrow," Merry said. "What time is the service?"

Ivy's eyes widened. "You'll go with me?"

"Sure, Mom. I'm not a heathen. At least not yet."

Ivy laughed, and the happy sound floated through the kitchen, settling over Merry. The peacefulness lasted for a moment until Merry glanced out the window. A Jeep pulled up to the backdoor, and Wise Man Joe hopped out.

"What's he doing here?" Merry grumbled and hurried upstairs.

Talking to the wise man for the third time today wasn't on her to-do list.

Chapter Nine

Merry waited upstairs until Wise Man Joe left. She watched his Jeep back out of their driveway and then padded down the stairs to find her mom. "Is he gone?" she asked.

"Yes. Why did you disappear? I wanted to introduce you to him." Her mom looked up from scrubbing the table and smiled.

"Met him already, remember?" Merry shrugged. "Why did he stop again?"

"Wanted to make sure I got home safe." Ivy shrugged. "He's a nice young man. He lives on the old Dousman farm. He bought it four years ago. Four? I think so. Something like that."

"How often does he stop by?" Merry asked, narrowing her eyes.

"Now and then. Joe likes to check on me, and I appreciate his kindness. I feed him sometimes. He doesn't have any family around here. They live a couple of hours away." Ivy wrung out the washcloth and turned to Merry. "What do you want to eat? I can whip something up. Eggs? Grilled cheese?"

Merry wrinkled her nose and frowned. "I'm not hungry."

"You never were hungry when we traveled. How about chicken noodle soup?"

"Perfect," Merry said. "Do you mind if I go to bed early?"

"Of course not, sweetheart. I bet you're exhausted after that drive. We will catch up tomorrow." Ivy smiled a tight smile.

Merry sighed. She disappointed her mom and knew it, but she wasn't ready for chit-chat. *I should have stayed in Atlanta.* She sighed and rested her head on her hands.

"Would you rather head to bed and skip the soup?" Mom asked from the stove.

Merry shook her head. "No, but I'm sorry I'm such bad company tonight."

"No worries, dear. You'll feel better in the morning." Ivy poured the hot soup into a bowl and set it in front of Merry. "You always loved a bowl of chicken noodle soup. It fixed all your woes."

Merry rolled her eyes. "I must have been a dumb kid, Mom."

A shadow crossed Ivy's eyes, and she sighed. "Merry, I wish you wouldn't talk that way about yourself."

"I know, Mom. I know. I'll stop." Merry slurped the soup and kissed her mother's cheek. "I'm going to get some sleep, and I'll try to muster some cheer for tomorrow. Okay?"

Ivy nodded and kissed Merry's cheek. "I love you, Merry Noel."

Merry nodded and hurried up the stairs.

Merry slid between the blankets in her chilly bedroom. *What kind of person doesn't say I love you to their mother?* "Apparently, a person like me," Merry whispered in the dark. She rested on the pillow and inhaled. The room smelled of her childhood—woodstove, homemade laundry detergent, and a mix of coffee and food. The paneled walls of her room held posters she'd slapped up in the 1990s. The faces of her favorite boy band watched over her from the wall with faded cheesy grins.

Merry rolled her eyes, thinking of her teenage self. Young Merry had big dreams to join a band and sing backup. She also wanted to marry a rich man and sail around the world in his yacht while servants cared for the chores. Old Merry lay in her childhood room, wondering where it all went wrong. Her ambition and dreams had fled, and she'd settled for a job she hated in a city that she had to convince herself she loved.

She sighed and closed her eyes. She doubted things would seem better in the morning, but she'd never know if she didn't fall asleep soon.

Sun streamed through Merry's window, and she groaned. Frost painted pictures on her window, and her breath blew out in wispy puffs. She burrowed under the blankets and squeezed her eyes shut. She'd forgotten this part—the shivering and freezing in the morning. Either her mom wasn't awake yet to add wood to the fire, or it was extra cold outside this morning.

Merry mustered the courage to jump out of bed and shrieked when her feet touched the icy floor. She grabbed her suitcase and ran down to the living room. She'd dress by the stove and plant her body in front of the warmth until returning to a normal human temperature.

She added logs to the fire and spread her sweater and jeans in front of the stove. The heat warmed her skin, and she smiled as her frozen body thawed. She reached for her sweater and heard the back door slam. "Mom?" she called, slipping her arms into the sweater and grabbing her jeans.

"It's Joe," a voice called from the kitchen. "I stopped to check on you before heading to church this morning. Need a ride?"

Merry shrieked and ran to the stairway before Wise Man Joe stepped into the living room and caught her warming by the fire.

"Sorry. Didn't mean to surprise you," Wise Man Joe hollered.

Merry slid her feet into slippers and hurried to the kitchen. "I don't know where my mom is, but I don't need a ride. Thanks." She eyed Wise Man Joe coolly, then asked, "Do you always walk into my mother's house? Don't you knock?"

Joe smiled, and his eyes twinkled. Merry shifted uncomfortably at the kindness oozing from his gaze.

"No one knocks in Liberty Ridge, but I'll try to remember to knock while you're visiting. Forgive me?" Joe held out a hand, and Merry raised her chin, staring at him until he dropped his hand to his side.

The screen door creaked shut, and Ivy came in carrying a basket of eggs and several pieces of wood. Joe grabbed the wood from her arms and carried the logs to the bin in the living room.

Merry watched the smooth movements and Mom's slight smile. *Just what exactly is going on here?*

"Will you stay for breakfast, Joe?" Ivy asked.

Joe shook his head. "No, thank you. I just stopped to check if you'd like a ride to church."

"We'll go this evening to the Christmas Eve service. Thanks for checking." She patted her hair and smoothed her apron. Her cheeks turned pink as she smiled.

Merry glanced back and forth between the two, unsure of what she had witnessed, but she didn't like it. Not one bit.

Chapter Ten

Merry moved around the kitchen in silence. She poured a cup of coffee, flipped a pancake before it burned, and glanced toward the back door, watching her mother and Wise Man Joe giggle together. A muscle in the back of Merry's neck tightened, and she clenched her jaw.

"Let's see. Where was I?"

Merry watched her mother breeze into the kitchen, her eyes sparkling, and a rosy blush crept up her cheeks.

"Oh good, you flipped that one. Are you hungry for one or two pancakes today?" She held the spatula and a plate and smiled.

"One," Merry said as she massaged her tight neck.

Ivy frowned. "Your neck hurting? Did you sleep funny last night, honey?"

"No," Merry said. "Just a kink. I'm fine."

"Well, sit down and eat. Warm enough?"

Merry sat at the table and pulled the blanket around her shoulders. She wore wool socks and slippers on her feet and a sweater over her sweatshirt. "Oh, sure, Mom." Merry rolled her eyes. "I'm toasty."

Ivy laughed. "I guess you've grown accustomed to warmer weather. Your blood probably thinned out."

"Something like that," Merry said and took a big gulp of coffee. "Why didn't you go to church with Wise Man Joe?"

Ivy smiled and patted Merry's arm. "I wanted to stay home and visit with my baby girl. Besides, you promised to go with me tonight, and I didn't think you'd go this morning too."

"You got me there, Mom." Merry chewed a bite of pancake and sighed. "These are delicious."

"Thanks, sweetheart." Her mom smiled, and Merry knew she wanted to say something. Something Merry didn't want to hear. She jumped up from the table and added a log to the woodstove. "I'm going to make my bed, Mom," she called from the living room and hurried up the stairs before her mother replied.

Merry straightened her old room quickly. The heat from the wood stove didn't quite reach her room, and she remembered childhood days when she'd set her clothes in the chair near the woodstove before bed. Every morning, she'd wrap herself in a blanket and race down to dress in front of the stove. *If I didn't have to worry about Wise Man Joe coming and going, I might dress down there again.*

Merry shook her head, unable to forget the look between her mom and Joe. She hurried down to the warmth and glanced out the window. Snowflakes swirled around her mom as she rushed to the barn, carrying her basket. Merry smiled and sank into the corner of the couch, pulling the afghan around her shoulders. She picked up the book on the coffee table and glanced through the pages to decide if she should read or rest her eyes.

Reading in front of a cozy fire on a snowy Wisconsin Christmas Eve seemed like a good idea—something straight from one of those cheesy movies Mom loved.

“Reading it is,” Merry whispered and opened to the first chapter. She read several minutes before Mom returned.

The back door creaked open, and Ivy stomped her feet. “Goodness, it’s windy out there,” she said.

Merry glanced out the picture window. Snow swirled around the yard, falling in big flakes. The sky, a mix of clear and gray, promised a storm soon. “Is it supposed to storm, Mom?”

“I think so,” Mom’s voice drifted from the kitchen. “Throw another log in the stove. I’ll sit with you and drink my coffee for a bit.”

Merry added wood to the fire and waited for her mom. "Where do you want to sit? I think I took your spot," she said and held up the book she'd found on the table.

Ivy waved Merry back to the couch. "I'm fine over here," she said and dropped into a recliner near the fire. "I must say, I'm so happy to have you here for Christmas." A smile lit her face, and Merry's heart clenched.

She smiled. "I'm glad you're happy, Mom."

Ivy leaned her head back on the chair, her eyes closed. "I'm going to lie down a bit before lunch. Make yourself comfortable, Merry."

Merry frowned. "Are you all right, Mom?" She couldn't remember her mother resting in the morning—late afternoon once in a while, but never in the morning.

"Of course, I'm fine, Merry. Just tired. I don't have as much energy these days, and the cold seems to wear me down a bit faster than it used to. That's all." She smiled. "I'll rest an hour, and then you can help me prepare lunch. I might make another batch of Christmas cookies too."

Merry nodded and curled up on the couch. A nap sounded like the perfect way to spend Christmas Eve.

Chapter Eleven

Merry jumped when the back door opened. The sky had darkened, and Merry blinked hard. *How long was I asleep?* She rubbed her eyes and stood, glancing out the window. The wind blew snow in gusts, and the flakes swirled around the house, rattling the windows.

"It's pretty bad out there. I don't think we will make it to Christmas Eve service."

Merry turned from the window to the man in the kitchen. *Wise Man Joe again?* "Why do you say that? Mom's counting on going."

Joe unwrapped his scarf, dropping clumps of snow on the floor. Merry stared at the mess and back at Joe.

He chuckled. "Don't worry. I'll clean that up before Miss Ivy ever sees the mess. Where is she? I wanted to get her opinion on what we should do."

Merry glanced around. "She's not in the kitchen? She must still be resting. I'll find her."

Merry knocked on her mother's bedroom door. "Mom, Joe's here."

Ivy opened the door and patted her hair. "I was lying there considering warming up the soup and fell back to sleep. Sorry, sweetheart." She reached and patted Merry's cheek.

Merry shrugged. "I don't mind, Mom. I just woke up myself when that wildebeest slammed the back door."

"Wildebeest? Merry Noel, you be nice."

"Why does he come in without knocking?"

Ivy shrugged. "He's a nice young man, honey. He helps me around here with ..." She stopped and sighed. "Well, with all the things I can't handle since your dad ..."

Merry cut her off. “He’s waiting.”

Wise Man or Wildebeest Joe sat near the fire warming his hands. He stood when the women entered the room. “Ivy, I stopped by to offer you a ride to Christmas Eve service, but my truck had difficulty getting here from next door. I don’t think we should go on into town in this weather. I’m sorry. I know you love the Christmas Eve service.”

Ivy sighed. “Well, I love the candles and the songs, but it’s not worth getting killed or stranded. We can have service ourselves. I have candles. Will you stay, Joseph?”

Ivy dug through cupboards, setting candles on the counter. “You know, Merry, we have all those lovely Christmas records. Why don’t you put one on to set the mood for our Christmas Eve dinner?” She smiled at Merry in that unique mom way that meant, “I’m not asking.”

Merry turned to the living room and bumped into the wildebeest. He held up his hands and grinned. “If you want to dance, just say so.” He laughed a deep laugh, and Merry frowned, pushing away from him.

That man is a bore.

She dug out Christmas albums and plugged in her mom's record player. The sounds of her least favorite song, "White Christmas" floated through the space, and Merry cranked the volume to cover the sound of mother and Joe laughing in the kitchen. Her mom stepped into the living room, drying her hands on a dishtowel.

"Sweetheart, put on that church choir record. We should save Bing until we read the Scripture and pray together." She raised her eyebrows and smiled. "Okay?"

Merry nodded and wondered at the rosy cheeks and sparkle in her mom's eye. She didn't like this one bit. Who was this man, and why did he insist on spending so much time with her mother? She'd get to the bottom of this mess. She had a sinking feeling he intended to steal the farm from her mom or worse yet—. Her stomach lurched, and she swallowed the bile that rose in her throat. She wouldn't say *that* out loud much less think it. Merry dug out the choir record, adjusted the volume to the perfect setting, and joined the festivities in the kitchen.

Ivy stood at the stove, warming soup and stirring milk for cocoa. Joe sliced bread at the counter. "Merry, please find the butter and set the table."

Merry scurried around the kitchen, obeying her mom. She spread the Christmas tablecloth, lit candles, and dug out her mother's Christmas china.

Joe glanced out the window. "It's getting worse."

"You might have to spend the night."

Merry whipped her head around and gawked at her mother. *Is she flirting with him? Oh, my word.*

Merry stared a moment when Joe held his hand out to her, but grabbed it. His large hand enclosed hers, and the feel of his warm touch sent shivers down her spine. She peeked while he prayed. Her mother's head bowed nearly to her chest. Her gray hair sparkled in the candlelight, and she had wrinkles in the corner of her eyes that Merry hadn't noticed the last time she'd come home. Joe prayed on and on—-something about health and safety and the storm. *Blah blah blah.* Merry glanced in his direction and decided his prayer seemed sincere. His dark hair curled with a slight wave, and Merry felt an urge to run her fingers through it. She cleared her throat at the thought. *What is wrong with me? Is that why Mom lets him keep coming around? He's cute?* Merry sighed. *What am I going to do with you, Mother?*

"Amen," Ivy said. "Pass the butter, please, Merry. I'm famished." She smiled at Merry and held out her hand for the china dish. "I don't suppose you get good butter down there in Atlanta, sweetheart. Spread it thick on that bread and enjoy. It's Christmas."

"Atlanta?" Joe asked. "Did you catch any baseball games?"

Merry shook her head and dug into the beef and barley soup, ignoring his question.

"Merry's a busy girl. Aren't you, Merry?"

Merry nodded.

"Too busy to make it up to cold Wisconsin often, so this visit is a special treat." Her mom reached over and patted her arm. Merry smiled.

Merry glanced around the kitchen. Candles flickered on the table, and Merry remembered other Christmas Eves when she and her parents ate soup at this table—with these candles and that music. A lump rose in her throat, and she attempted to swallow it away, but then the back of her eyes stung, and she knew she'd cry in thirty seconds or less. She jumped up from the table. "Excuse me, I forgot my gas tablets," she said and fled from the room.

I forgot my gas tablets? My GAS tablets. Merry Noel, you are a moron. When she needed to flee before the tears started, she'd said the first thing that crossed her mind. Now she sat on the edge of her bed with flaming red cheeks and stinging eyes. *I will* not *cry right now. I don't have time for a headache.*

She blew out a breath and stood to pace around her room. She took several deep breaths, squared her shoulders, and opened her door. How she'd face Wise Man Joe after announcing her non-existent gas problem, she didn't know, but she knew Mother would come looking for her soon.

Joe looked up when she returned to the kitchen. "You okay, Miss Merry?" His eyes twinkled, and his shoulders shook.

She shot him a withering stare, and he winked. *I never!* She plopped in a chair and grabbed her napkin, keeping her eyes on the bowl of soup. The sky had darkened when she went on her made-up errand and the kitchen seemed cozier. The candles flickered and added a peaceful feeling to the room, but the wind howled. Merry shivered.

Ivy leaned over and patted her. "When did you start having gas problems, sweetie? Probably all that stress. You need some of my kombucha to get your gut healthy."

"Mom!" she exclaimed. "I'm fine."

Ivy nodded and passed the bread. "Eat up."

The music finished playing, and Merry listened to the scratch of the blank spot on the record. It reminded her of days gone by, and she swallowed fast before the lump returned.

"After cleaning up the kitchen," Ivy said, "we can read the Nativity story and share our favorite Christmas memories. Then maybe a game of Yahtzee and more hot cocoa before bed. Might as well make the best of the storm."

She cleared the table, and Joe jumped to help.

"I'll find Dad's Bible and turn the record player off," Merry said.

"Set it up to play Bing after we read, honey," Ivy called.

Merry swallowed hard to ward off that pesky lump. She found her father's Bible on the shelf and sat in his chair near the woodstove. Her fingers rubbed the smooth spot on the cover, and she closed her eyes. If she concentrated, she could almost hear his deep voice reading, "And it came to pass in those days, that there went out a decree from Caesar Augustus that all the world should be taxed ..."

She opened her eyes and glanced around the room. Everything looked as it had when she grew up, and Merry wondered if she could fool herself into believing that everything remained the same.

Chapter Twelve

"Oh, there you are, sweetie." Ivy wiped her hands on a dishcloth and tightened her red and green Christmas apron strings. "We're starting Yahtzee. Want to play a round or two?" She stood in the doorway with her hands on her hips and a cheerful smile on her lips.

Merry rubbed the Bible cover once more and stood. "Of course, Mom. It's been a while since I've beaten anyone at Yahtzee."

Ivy snapped the dish towel at Merry and laughed. "Oh, I don't know about that, my dear. I'm pretty good at that game. Come on in and get settled at the table. I'm warming more milk for cocoa to keep the cold out of our bones."

Merry sat across from her mother, which meant she sat a little too close for comfort to Joe. She pulled her feet together in front of her chair and kept her elbows close to her sides. She didn't want any more touches from his strong hand, and she didn't want to smell that amazing cologne he wore either. *Stop acting like an idiot, Merry. Pull yourself together.*

Joe grabbed the dice and the cup. "Guests go first." He laughed, and Merry smirked. As much as she hated admitting it, she liked the guy. He was friendly and cheerful, and while she wondered why he spent so much time with her mother, she dropped a couple of the guards surrounding her heart and decided to at least behave civilly.

He rolled the dice and got a full house on his first try.

Merry shook her head. "Oh, it's on now," she said.

They played several rounds of Yahtzee and drank too many cups of hot cocoa. The cozy kitchen settled Merry's mind, and her eyes drooped.

Ivy slapped the table. "Well, children. Old Ivy won again. It's time to put this away and get the Christmas story read. It's almost midnight." She glanced out the window and frowned. "Looks like you're staying here, Joe." She stepped to the window and pressed her face to the glass. "Yep, snow's already past your front bumper."

He peered out the window and whistled. "I didn't hear the weather report say to prepare for this much snow. I hope the storm slows down soon." He rubbed his arms and shivered.

"It reminds me of the *Long Winter* when the Ingalls had to twist hay to burn to stay warm. If we have to go out tomorrow, we'll have to tie a line back to the house, so we don't lose anyone," Ivy said.

Merry chuckled. "I loved those books, but you're right. That whistling wind makes me shiver. Good thing we don't have to fight for survival like they did."

"Amen to that," Joe said. "Shall we, ladies?" He stood in the doorway and moved to the living room.

Merry followed him and plopped on the sofa. She curled up in the corner and pulled the afghan around her. Her tired eyes drooped; the crackling fire and warm room relaxed her tense muscles.

"Joe, would you read for us?" Ivy handed the Bible to him, and Merry frowned.

Dad's Bible, really?

Joe held the Bible between his large hands and bowed his head. "Thank you, Ivy, for asking me to do this. Should we pray first?"

Ivy nodded, and Merry looked away as her mother settled into the chair next to Joe.

"'... But Mary kept all these things and pondered them in her heart. And the shepherds returned, glorifying and praising God for all the things that they had heard and seen, as it was told unto them.'" Joe closed the Bible and patted the cover. "I always wonder what the people thought when the shepherds returned and told their news. Did you ever think about the parts of the story the Bible left out?"

Ivy nodded. "I always consider Mary and her pondering."

"Ponder is a good word," Joe said. "Something all of us should do with the Bible."

Merry sat up from the corner of the couch and frowned. "You left out your part of the story."

Joe frowned. "My part?"

"The wise men," Merry said.

"Oh," Joe laughed. "You mean my costume from the Jingle Mingle? The wise men are in Matthew's account. You know they weren't at the manger?"

Merry scowled. "Really? I never heard that."

"Here, let me read the passage." He flipped through the pages of her father's Bible and read. "'When they had heard the king, they departed; and, lo, the star, which they saw in the east, went before them, till it came and stood over where the young child was. When they saw the star, they rejoiced with exceeding great joy. And when they were come into the house, they saw the young child with Mary, his mother, and fell down, and worshipped him: and when they had opened their treasures, they presented unto him gifts; gold, and frankincense, and myrrh.'"

Ivy nodded her head. "Jesus was a child, and they lived in a house."

Merry frowned. "Well, why are they always in the manger scene?"

Joe shrugged. "Maybe for convenience. I mean, they *are* part of the story."

Merry stood and folded the afghan. "Well, that's enough new information for me for one evening. I'm beat." She stretched.

"Joe, do you want the couch or the guest room at the top of the stairs?" Ivy asked.

"Guest room is fine, Miss Ivy. Thank you. I would have stayed home if I knew the storm would turn so quickly. I should call my mom and let her know I might not make it home tomorrow."

Ivy frowned. "How will your mom feel about that?"

Joe laughed. "Don't you worry about my mom. My family is so large that I doubt she'll notice I'm missing. Thank you for putting me up tonight."

Ivy patted his arm. "It's not a problem at all, Joe. I'm glad you came over for games and cocoa, and I'm glad you're safe and snug here with us. I do hope the county will plow tomorrow. I don't mind being snowed in for Christmas, but I'd like to get to town eventually."

Merry shivered and scurried up the stairs. She hadn't lived through a white Christmas in years, but this Christmas made up for all the snowy Decembers she had missed.

"Good night, Miss Merry," Joe called.

"Good night, sweetheart," her mom's voice floated up the stairs. Merry shut the door and burrowed under the quilts, trying to erase the picture of her mom and Joe grinning at each other.

Chapter Thirteen

Merry huddled under the quilt and watched the storm howl outside her window. Her mind raced while the frigid wind whirling outside settled in her bones. Her teeth chattered. She pulled the extra blanket over her and closed her eyes, but her mind wouldn't shut down.

She hadn't celebrated Christmas at home for years, and this one seemed extra Christmasy with the blizzard. Her eyes popped open when the shutter banged against the house. She lay in bed, watching the storm, and tried to sort all the thoughts bouncing around in her exhausted mind.

She'd need a job soon, and who knows what kind of reference her boss would give after her hissy fit at the office party. If she moved from Atlanta, she had to sell her condo. If she didn't get a job, her bank account would scream before long, and then what?

She threw the covers off and padded to the window. She scratched the icy film with her fingernail and whispered, "They say you can't go home, yet here I am." She jumped when the shutter banged against the house. "Someone needs to fix that thing."

Merry grabbed the quilt and tiptoed downstairs. She couldn't sleep. Maybe sitting by the warm woodstove would calm her and cause her eyes to droop. The bottom stair creaked, and Merry grimaced. She used to expertly tiptoe down the stairs and sneak out to parties when she was younger. "You're losing it in your old age, Mer," she whispered.

Joe had packed the woodstove full of logs before turning in. The fire crackled and filled the room with heat. Merry held her hands in front of the stove to warm her fingers. The frame on the bookshelf near her mom's chair sparkled in the firelight. Merry rubbed her thumb across the glass. "Daddy," she whispered. "I miss you."

A wave of grief rolled over Merry, and she choked back a sob. She blew out her breath and looked down at her father's smiling face. The back of her eyes burned, but she wouldn't give in. Merry Noel didn't have time for crying. She was strong and capable. Crying didn't change a thing. She swallowed hard, reached for the photo album, and plopped down in her daddy's chair. Wrapping the quilt around her shoulders, she flipped through the pages.

Merry wrapped head to toe like a mummy, ready for sledding.

Daddy pushing her on the swing.

Mom and Merry on the steps in pastel Easter dresses.

Daddy leaning in her car window, telling her to drive safely.

Merry rubbed her thumb over every photo of her father. The lump in her throat grew too big to swallow. She blinked and rubbed her eyes. The flames danced behind the glass, and if Merry didn't know better, the cozy room appeared to shelter happy memories and good times. She turned the page in the photo album and gasped. She threw the album across the room and fell to the ground in a heap while sobs wracked her body.

A bedroom door creaked open, and footsteps marched across the room. "What in the ...?" her mom trailed off and sunk to the floor, nestling against Merry's side. "Merry? Sweetie?"

Mother's arms pulled her close, and Merry leaned into her side. Mom patted her back and wrapped the quilt around Merry while clucking her tongue and whispering, "There now. It's okay. Let it out."

Footsteps hurried down the stairs, and Ivy shook her head against Merry's hair. The footsteps marched back up, and a door clicked shut.

"What brought this on?"

Merry blinked and attempted to swallow the lump in her throat. Hot tears ran down her cheeks, and her chest ached. She opened her mouth, but nothing came out. She tried to breathe as sobs shook her body.

"Do you know what I think, Miss Merry Noel?" her mom whispered into her hair.

"What?" Merry whispered.

"I think that Merry Noel doesn't hate Christmas. No, for all her pretending and staying away and her Ebenezer Scrooge act, I don't believe for a moment that my sweet girl hates Christmas."

"I do," Merry croaked over the lump in her raw throat.

"No, ma'am. You do not."

"Don't tell me what I don't hate, Mother," Merry whispered.

Ivy leaned down and kissed Merry's forehead and smoothed her hair. "You don't hate Christmas, Merry. You hate what happened at Christmas."

Merry whispered, "I loathe Christmas."

"Merry, you need to face your grief. It's time. Were you looking at pictures?"

Merry nodded.

"Is that what you threw?"

Merry nodded again.

"Looking at happier times hurts, doesn't it?" Ivy whispered. "But remembering the good times is important. God blessed us with your daddy."

Merry swallowed hard, but the sob burst out and shook her. She leaned into her mother and tried to catch a breath, but her tears flowed in a torrent of grief. Ivy patted her back and smoothed her hair.

"Your daddy tried to stay alive past Christmas. Did you know that?"

Merry wiped her nose on her sleeve. Her eyes burned, and still, the tears flowed. Her breath came in short gasps, and her heart pounded.

"He said, 'I don't want to ruin the holiday for Merry.' You always loved Christmas." Ivy sniffled and wiped her eyes. "I wanted to keep him longer, you know, and he wanted to stay. He worried about me and you—you most of all. You were always daddy's baby."

Merry melted into her mother's side and sobbed, wiping her eyes and cheeks on the quilt. She dropped the soggy corner on her lap and blew out a shaky breath. "Oh, Mom," she said, and the sobs started again.

"Losing someone you love is never easy. It hurts," Ivy whispered. "But you have to feel those feelings and work through them. You ran away, Merry. I knew that's what you were doing. Especially when you refused to come home for Christmas." Her voice quivered, and she took a deep breath. "I waited for you. Every year, I prayed you'd come home. You were always too busy, but I knew what you were doing. You were avoiding the pain, weren't you?"

Merry nodded.

"That's not healthy, darling. Grief will break you if you don't let it out. What changed this year?" Ivy sat up and nudged Merry. She held Merry's chin and gazed into her eyes. "Why did you come home now?"

Merry hiccupped as she blew out a breath. "I got fired," she whispered.

"Oh, Merry, I'm sorry, but not really. I'm glad you're here. I'm even glad you're sobbing on my living room floor, soaking my favorite quilt. It was time," she whispered.

"Why did you take those pictures of him when he was sick?" Merry whispered.

Ivy sat still for several moments. "I'm not sure, Merry. I've wondered that myself. He looks awful when I look at the pictures now. But at the moment, he just looked like my high-school sweetheart, and I wanted to remember."

"I should get back to bed," Merry whispered.

Ivy kissed the top of her head. "I'm glad you're home, Merry. You can stay as long as you like."

Merry smiled and kissed her mother's cheek. "That storm is a doozy," she said.

The snow whirled outside the window and whistled through the cracks of the old farmhouse. The shutter slammed against the house, and Merry jumped. "You need to ask Wise Man Joe to fix that shutter for you, Mom," Merry said.

Ivy laughed and untangled herself from her daughter. "I'll see what he can do when the weather calms down. Let me grab you a Tylenol. Your head will ache in the morning after all these tears."

The shutter banged again, this time more forceful. Merry frowned. “Mom?” she called. “I don’t think that’s the shutters.”

Chapter Fourteen

Ivy stepped into the living room with the pain reliever and a frown on her face. “Why do you say that?”

“I don’t know, but the noise was different.” She shrugged. “Who knows? I’m tired, and it’s late.”

The noise banged again, and Ivy’s eyes widened. “That’s definitely not the shutters.” She peered out the front window. “All I see is the snow. Maybe someone’s dog got loose.” She reached for the doorknob.

“Mom! Stop. What if it’s not a dog? I mean, knocking on doors in the middle of a blizzard sounds exactly like something a serial killer would do."

Ivy laughed. "Oh, honey, nothing exciting ever happens around this sleepy town. It's either a dog or someone's Christmas decorations blowing into our door. I assure you there's not a person on the other side of this door." She tugged the heavy door open, and she and Merry gasped.

"Mom, that is definitely not a dog."

"No, it is not. Come help me," Ivy called.

The wind howled around the snug farmhouse and blew snow inside the door. Merry shivered and ran to help her mom lift the collapsed pile from the porch.

Ivy whispered and slid her arms underneath the arms on the bundle. "Come on. Help me out here. Can you stand?"

Merry slid her arm around the bundle, and she and her mother lifted. The person unfolded from the porch and stood on thin, shaky legs.

"Here you go. One foot in front of the other. You can do it," Ivy encouraged. Merry held onto the bundle and helped steer. "Let's put her in my bed."

"How do you know it's a her?" Merry whispered.

Ivy shook her head and pointed to her bedroom. Chunks of cold snow fell off the bundle as they shuffled across the room, and Merry shivered. The women managed to get the girl to lie down on Ivy's bed. "Get blankets," her mother ordered. "And more logs on the fire. Hurry."

Merry ran to obey her mother's orders as Ivy pulled the shoes off the bundle. Merry ran in with a pile of blankets and stopped at the door. Her eyes widened when Ivy unbuttoned the coat. "Is she ...?"

Ivy nodded. "And by the looks of this girl, it's almost showtime."

Merry slumped against the door frame and covered her face with her hands. She blew out a deep breath as nausea rolled through her stomach.

"Merry!" Ivy barked. "I do not have time for you to get squeamish. Wake up Joe and get him down here."

Merry frowned. "What's he going to do?"

Ivy's eyes widened, and she pointed at Merry. "He's a paramedic. Hurry."

Merry took the stairs two at a time and pounded on the guest room door. Her heart hammered in her chest, and her head buzzed. How in the world was this happening on Christmas Eve of all nights? She pounded again and yelled, "Joe, Mom needs you."

The door crashed open, and Joe stood in front of Merry, stuffing his arms into a flannel shirt. Merry tried to look away from his muscled chest, rapidly disappearing behind buttons. Her cheeks flushed, and she blew out a breath to clear her mind.

"What did you say?" Joe asked, his tousled hair standing on end, giving him the appearance of a little boy—other than those muscles.

"Mom needs you downstairs. Hurry."

Joe grabbed a bag and ran past her and down the stairway, calling, "Ivy? What is it?"

Merry followed behind and squeezed into the bedroom to hear her mother say, “She’s at a nine already.”

Merry grimaced. A nine? “What’s a nine?” she asked, glancing between them.

“A nine means it’s almost baby time,” Joe said. He sat on the side of the bed and held the thin wrist. He counted, pulled a stethoscope out of his bag, and placed the bell on her chest.

When had he grabbed a stethoscope? “I’m losing my grip on reality,” she whispered. “I’m dreaming, right? This is all just a dream. You need to wake up, Merry.”

The bundle in the bed groaned and turned on her side. Nope. Not a dream.

Ivy smoothed the girl’s hair and whispered. “We’re going to help you. You’re safe.”

“Where did she come from?” Joe asked. He adjusted the blankets and examined the girl’s eyes.

“We heard a noise and thought the shutters were loose at first. Merry thought I was letting in a serial killer,” Ivy teased. Her eyes sparkled, and she grinned at Merry.

Merry shrugged. "Hey, too many movies. I never expected this." She pointed at the bed, and the girl groaned.

"Merry, find me several towels and boil some water," Joe ordered.

"I thought boiling water was a myth."

"Please," Joe said.

The woman screamed and twisted on the bed.

"We're here," Ivy said. "You're in good hands. What's your name?"

"Angel," the girl gasped.

"Hold on, Angel, you're in good hands," Ivy said as Merry hurried to follow orders as the girl groaned again.

She ran to the kitchen, filled pots with water, and cranked the stove burners on high. She slammed cupboard doors and dropped pans onto the stove with extra energy to drown out the woman's groans. Merry's stomach lurched at each one, and her eyes widened. "Please don't let the baby die," Merry whispered. "Not on Christmas. No more death on Christmas." A tear slipped down her cheek.

Eight years ago, on Christmas morning, her father had closed his eyes and lost his battle with cancer. The tree lights sparkled, and a choir belted out carols on the record player in the corner when the paramedics came to carry her father to the funeral home. Smelling pine or hearing cheerful Christmas music still had the power to reduce Merry to a puddle of tears. "It's too hard," she whispered. She scooped coffee into the filter and added an extra tablespoon before turning on the pot. She leaned against the counter and blinked her eyes, trying to chase away images of the paramedics wheeling her covered father past the wreath on the front door.

"Merry, towels!" Joe shouted.

Merry ran to the linen closet, grabbed the stack of mismatched towels, and hurried into the bedroom as the girl groaned. Merry held out the towels, her eyes wide.

"Whoa," she said. The scene was nothing she'd ever witnessed. Joe sat near the woman's legs, and Ivy held the woman's hand and whispered in her ear. "Is that ...? Is she

…?" Merry asked. "Why don't you give her something for the pain?"

Joe grabbed the pile of towels. "She's doing great. I don't have anything to give her that will help. This part isn't fun, but there's no way to birth a baby without going through the process."

Merry watched for a moment, but her head swam, and her stomach twisted. So much blood and misery. She covered her eyes and peeked between her fingers.

"Why don't you wait out there?" Joe pointed to the living room, and Merry turned and ran. The twinkling tree lights and the scent of pine crashed over her in a wave, and she dropped into her father's chair, choking back a sob.

Chapter Fifteen

Merry sat frozen in her father's chair. The noises in the other room rang in her ears, and her stomach twisted. She tapped her feet on the floor and gripped the arms of the chair. Her breath came in gasps like the girl in her mother's bed. She prayed the only words she could string together, "God, help that baby live. Please."

The girl screamed, and Merry jumped to her feet and paced. She stood outside the door and watched for a moment, but the woman's misery brought tears to her eyes. She stumbled backward and ran to the kitchen.

Merry sat at the table and covered her ears with her hands. Her prayer ran through her mind to the beat of her heart, and tears slipped down her cheeks. Why had she come home? Her painful memories and the absence of her father combined with the miserable girl on her mother's bed seemed too much to handle. *If a blizzard didn't rage out there, I'd drive straight back to Atlanta.* She smiled for a moment, thinking of how ridiculous running away would be in these conditions. Her mother's words from earlier echoed. *You have to go through the process, or grief will break you.* "Yeah, well, I don't want to go through this process."

"What did you say?" Joe stood at the coffee pot filling a mug. He leaned on the counter and smiled.

Merry jumped up. "Is Angel okay?"

"Yes, everything is fine. She's progressing normally."

"Then why aren't you in there? Help her!" Merry yelled, the panic rising in her chest.

"Whoa, Merry, it's all right. She's doing great. I think the baby will be here in the next hour or two," Joe said as he stirred the cream into his mug.

"An hour?" Merry dropped into the chair and rested her head on the table. "Ugh."

Joe sat in the chair next to her and rested his hand on her arm. "Merry, take a deep breath. Why are you so worked up?"

Merry glanced up into his kind eyes and gulped. "Because ..." She let out the breath she held, and a sob escaped.

"Hey." Joe patted her arm. "It's all right. The baby is truly okay, and so is Angel. Don't worry. I've done this before."

"You've delivered a baby before?" Merry asked.

Joe winked. "A time or two." He rinsed the coffee mug and smiled at Merry. "It's quite miraculous. Should I call you when it's time?"

Merry's eyes widened, and she shook her head. Joe laughed and disappeared into her mother's bedroom. When a groan loud enough to shake the rafters echoed from her mom's bedroom, Merry dropped her head and whispered her prayer repeatedly to crowd out her worries about everything that could go wrong.

"Merry Noel, quick," Ivy called.

Merry jumped to her feet and hurried through the house. She skidded to a stop inside the door to the room and waited. Angel had thrown all the blankets off, and her wet hair was tangled around her face. "What do you need, Mom?" Merry whispered. She wanted to look away but couldn't peel her eyes off the scene.

"I want you to see this." Ivy pointed to the bed. "To see the miracle of life happening on this night. I want you to have some happy memories of Christmas Eve."

Merry gasped and stepped back. "I ... I don't know. Mom?" She stepped back into the hallway, gasping.

"Merry, try. I think you'll be sorry if you don't stay," Ivy said. She reached her hand to Merry and smiled. "Come."

Merry stepped into the room and stood in the corner. The volume in the room had changed, and Merry watched as Angel closed her eyes. "I can't do this anymore," she whispered.

"That's good, Angel. When you think you can't do it anymore, the baby is almost here. You've got this," Joe said.

Ivy smoothed Angel's hair and gripped her hand. "Ready, sweetheart. Your baby is almost here. Do you know what you're having?"

Angel groaned. "No," she gasped.

"Well, we're about to find out," Joe said.

Merry's eyes widened, and she pressed her back into the corner and bit her tongue. Joe and Mom didn't need her hyperventilating right now. *Keep it together, Merry. Now is not the time to fall apart. Although, if Joe had to give me mouth to mouth ...* She blushed at the unwanted thought. She still wasn't sure what Joe was to her mother and wasn't sure if she liked or trusted him. He seemed capable of delivering this baby—maybe he was okay.

Angel groaned, and Ivy patted her head and whispered in her ear. Joe stood and encouraged

Angel. "You've got this. You're doing it. Come on, Angel. Just one more push."

Joe grabbed the baby and slid a finger under the umbilical cord. He unwound it from the baby and rubbed the slippery body with a towel. "It's a girl," his deep voice cheered as he held the baby high for Angel to see. She smiled and lay back on the pillow. Ivy clapped her hands, and her eyes sparkled.

"Oh, Angel, she's beautiful," Ivy crooned.

Merry stood in the corner with tears pouring down her cheeks, and held her hand on her heart. The miracle she'd witnessed left her breathless and something else. Happy. She waited in the corner while Joe finished with the baby and handed her to Angel. Ivy leaned over the bed, cooing at the baby and patting Angel. She wiped away tears and glanced at Merry with a big smile.

Joe laid the baby in the crook of Angel's arm. "Good job, Momma." He patted her arm and sat back at the end of the bed to finish caring for Angel.

Angel whispered to the baby and pulled the towel around the little bundle.

Merry smiled and stood on her tiptoes to glimpse the chubby cheeks and dark tufts of hair escaping the towel. Her heart lurched, and tears poured down her face. The baby nestled into her mother and looked for something to eat. Ivy helped Angel and the baby find each other, and soon, the room filled with the contented sighs of the nursing baby.

Merry tiptoed from the room and sat in her father's chair. "Hey, Daddy," she whispered. "I don't know that I'll ever get over the pain of losing you. But after tonight, I don't loathe Christmas quite so much." She leaned back in the chair and watched the fire in the woodstove until her eyes drooped, and she fell asleep.

Chapter Sixteen

In the middle of the night, the house finally settled. Angel and the baby slept in Ivy's room. Joe had tiptoed to bed after watching Ivy tuck Angel in. Ivy had made a dark herbal tea and helped Angel drink the steaming concoction. She tucked her and the baby into bed and collapsed on the couch.

"Mom, why don't you sleep in my bed? I can listen and call you if Angel needs anything," Merry said.

Ivy sighed. "Good idea, but I'm too exhausted to move. I'll stay here, but I'd appreciate you listening for them, dear. I may sleep too deeply to hear anything."

"I can do that for you." Merry pulled the blanket around her and curled up in her father's chair. The excitement of the evening and the crackling fire lulled Merry into a deep sleep.

A floorboard creaked, and Merry's groggy eyes fluttered open. She glanced around the room and frowned. "Angel?"

Angel froze at the front door.

"What are you doing? Do you need a drink or help to the bathroom?" Merry asked.

Angel shook her head.

Merry jumped up from the chair. "Let's get you back to bed then." She crossed the living room to Angel and reached out to guide her back to the bedroom. "I don't want you to get cold."

Angel pulled her arm away from Merry's hand. A flash sparked in her eyes, and she frowned. "Leave me alone," she hissed.

Merry stepped back, and her eyes widened. "I'm sorry, Angel. I didn't mean to frighten you. I just don't want you to catch a chill and get sick."

Angel grabbed the doorknob and opened the front door. Frigid air whistled into the cozy living room, blowing in a pile of snow.

Merry wiped the snow from her shoulders. "Come, Angel. It's too cold to go out there." She reached for Angel's hand, but Angel pulled away and stepped toward the door.

"Please don't stop me." Her dark brown eyes warned Merry to step back, but something about Angel's demeanor alarmed Merry.

"Angel, it's too cold out there, and you just had a baby. You need to rest." Merry reached around Angel to shut the door, but Angel grabbed the handle and took another step toward the raging blizzard.

"I have to get out of here. He'll find me." Angel slapped a hand over her mouth, and her eyes widened.

"Who will find you?" Merry placed a hand on her hip and narrowed her eyes. "No one will find you in a blizzard, so you're safe for now. But who's after you? The baby's father?"

Angel nodded and grabbed the door handle, and Merry jumped to push against the door.

"No one is going anywhere in this storm. Do you understand me?" Merry frowned and gasped. "You left the baby?" Her jaw dropped.

"Please," Angel begged. "You have to let me go."

"You listen to me. You can't go anywhere in this storm. In your condition, that's non-negotiable."

Angel stared and reached around Merry for the doorknob. "Please," she begged. "You don't understand." Tears filled her eyes, and she grabbed for the door.

Merry leaned against the door to keep Angel from escaping. Angel grunted and strained to pull the door open.

"What is going on?" Ivy stood with her hands on her hips and a scowl on her face.

Merry pushed against the door. "Angel here planned to leave the baby and disappear into the blizzard. I'm trying to keep her inside."

Ivy stepped near the door. "Angel? You can't go out in this storm. You need to rest and get your strength back."

"I'm fine." Angel strained to pull the door open around Merry. "Leave me alone."

"She was going to leave the baby," Merry said.

Ivy frowned. "Angel? Is this true? If you leave the baby here, we have no way to feed her. The weather is too stormy to drive to town for baby formula."

Angel continued to struggle at the door, but a sob escaped. "Please, let me go. I have to get out of here before he ..."

"He who?" Joe's deep voice rumbled from across the room. He stood at the bottom of the stairs, buttoning his shirt.

Merry grinned at his tousled hair and five o'clock shadow. He even looked good half asleep.

He hurried across the room and joined Ivy. "What's going on, Angel? Let us help you."

A sob escaped from Angel, and she pulled at the doorknob. "Please," she begged. "You don't understand. Let me go."

Ivy stepped closer to the door and reached for Angel. "Come back to bed, Angel. When you rest, everything will look better."

Angel pulled away from Ivy's hand and grabbed the doorknob. She managed to pull the door open, and the wind whistled, blowing snow around the women. Merry leaned hard on the door and pushed it shut with a slam. Angel sank to the floor and sobbed.

"He's going to kill me," she cried.

Joe hurried to her side and pulled her up from the floor. "No one is killing anyone tonight. Not while I'm on watch. Come back to bed."

Ivy walked to the other side and supported Angel. "Your baby didn't even stir." Ivy smiled. "Look, she's all snuggled in. This little girl needs you, Angel. What will you name her?"

"Nothing," Angel whispered and turned to the wall, ignoring the baby lying in the box near the bed. Angel climbed into bed and turned away from the baby. Merry stood in the doorway, waiting for her mother to tuck Angel in. The baby snored a tiny whiffling snore, and a tear trickled down Angel's cheek.

Chapter Seventeen

Merry rested her head on her hands at the kitchen table. She wanted to sleep, but the evening's excitement kept her awake. Her brain buzzed even though the grit in her eyes screamed at her to go to bed.

Joe cleared his throat. "You okay, Miss Merry?"

Merry's head snapped up, and she blinked her tired eyes. "Yes, I'm fine. I can't sleep--too wound up. I didn't even do anything." She shrugged. "Coffee's fresh."

Joe smiled and sat in the chair across from her. "I should say no to any more caffeine, but I never sleep right away after assisting at a birth. Birthing babies is exciting and scary at the same time. Thankfully, Angel handled everything very well, and the birth was safe." He blew out a breath and wiped his bloodshot eyes. "I'm thankful because we couldn't get help here in time if something had gone wrong."

Merry grimaced. "Well, then, I'm thankful you were here to help her."

Joe smiled. "Part of the job."

"But you weren't on duty."

"That's true, but we are always on duty when needed," Joe said. "What do you think about her trying to sneak out into the storm?"

"I don't know. Why is Angel so afraid that she'd risk going into a blizzard hours after giving birth?" Merry rubbed her chin. "I wish we could help."

"Me too," Ivy said from the doorway. "Having a party without inviting me?" Her eyes twinkled, but she yawned. She patted Merry's arm. "Thanks for convincing Angel to stay safe inside."

"I don't think I convinced her, but I didn't let her leave. She'd die out there, wouldn't she?" Merry asked.

Joe nodded. "She'd risk her health. The snow is at least a foot deep out there, and I don't know how we'd find her if she had left."

"Who do you think she's running from?" Ivy asked.

"Do either of you recognize her from town?" Merry asked.

Joe and Ivy shook their heads, and Ivy frowned. "I don't recognize her, and she doesn't seem very old either. Seventeen?"

Joe nodded. "Something like that. I didn't ask."

Ivy yawned and covered her mouth. "Before I forget, I think we should take turns sitting up in case our new mama tries to sneak out into the storm again."

"I'll stay up for a few hours so you two can rest."

"Thank you, Joseph." Ivy reached over and squeezed his hand. "You're a good boy."

"I have an idea," Merry said. "Don't call me crazy until I spit everything out, even if I don't make sense? Okay?"

"Go ahead, honey," Ivy said and patted Merry's arm.

Joe nodded and gulped hot coffee. "Let's hear it." He leaned back in the chair and stretched.

Merry wrung her hands and stared at the table for a moment. She blew out a breath, and her idea tumbled out like a jingle bell rolling across the floor.

Ivy gasped, and her eyes shone with tears. "It's perfect. Absolutely perfect."

Joe dropped all four legs of the chair to the floor with a thud and stared.

"What?" Merry asked, defensiveness creeping into her voice.

He grinned. "Amazing." He stood and stretched. "You two go to bed and get some sleep. I'll watch Angel and the baby, and we'll talk in the morning. Sound good?"

"It's almost morning right now," Ivy said and laughed.

"Well, whenever everyone stirs," Joe said.

Ivy nodded, and Merry smiled. Her idea was crazy, but maybe it was crazy enough to work.

Merry sank into bed with a sigh and whispered a prayer as she dozed off. "Thank you, Lord, for giving me a happy memory for Christmas."

The sun stood high in the sky when Merry stirred. She glanced at the clock on the bedside table and groaned. "Ten o'clock." She sat up and shivered. The storm swirled snow outside her window, and cold air whistled through the worn window casings. Merry wrapped herself in a fuzzy pink bathrobe and stuffed her icy feet into the wool slippers.

"Mom," she called as she hurried downstairs. "Why didn't you wake me?"

"Shh," Ivy whispered. "You'll wake the baby."

Merry smiled and grabbed her mother in a hug. "Merry Christmas. You didn't open the presents without me, did you?"

Ivy swatted Merry and laughed. "Of course not, silly goose. I'm making cinnamon rolls. Joe is sleeping right now, and I'm on Angel alert. Come. Sit." She peeked at the rolls. "Ten minutes."

Merry filled one of her mom's Christmas mugs with coffee and plopped down at the table to wait for a fresh roll. "Did Angel sleep all night?"

"The baby wanted to nurse a couple of times, and they both fell back to sleep fairly fast. No more escape attempts."

Merry shivered. "What would possess her to leave safety to wander in a blizzard?"

Ivy shrugged and frowned. "We don't know what she's running from or facing at home, Merry. I assume she thought she had no other choice."

Merry reached for a roll from the pan Ivy had set on the table. She licked the gooey icing off of her fingers. "Thank you, Mom."

"For what?"

"For giving me a home that I didn't need to run from, even though I did. I'm sorry."

Ivy kissed her on top of her head. "You were running from your grief, not your mom. I knew it the whole time, but I sure missed you."

Merry wiped a tear away. "Grief is no joke, is it, Mom?"

Ivy shook her head. "No, it's not. It's awful, but it's part of life, and it's the price we pay for loving him so."

Merry swallowed over the lump growing in her throat. "I thanked God last night for giving me something happy to remember on Christmas Eve."

Ivy smiled and reached for Merry's hand. "Me too, honey."

Chapter Eighteen

"Let's check on the baby and Angel," Ivy said. Merry tiptoed behind her mother into the bedroom. Angel leaned against the pillows, smiling down at the dark-haired bundle, her eyes filled with tears.

Ivy stepped to the bed and patted Angel's hand. "How are you feeling this morning, Angel?"

Angel shrugged.

"Did you name baby yet?" she asked.

Angel turned her face away.

Joe cleared his throat behind Merry. "Good morning, Angel. Merry Christmas. How's that baby doing?"

Angel covered her face with her hands, and a tear rolled down her cheek.

Ivy patted Angel and reached for the baby. "Give me baby girl for a minute, and you get out of bed. Let's go sit by the fire and open our presents."

Angel frowned.

"Come on," Ivy said. "Don't argue with me. Everyone to the living room. I made cinnamon rolls."

Angel swung her legs out of bed, and Joe reached to help her stand.

A few moments later, the group had settled into the living room. Ivy held the baby in one arm and handed out cinnamon rolls. Joe filled mugs with steaming hot coffee, and Merry added logs to the fire.

"Turn the music on, Merry," Ivy said. "And plug in the Christmas tree lights, too."

They munched in silence as the voice of the Andrews Sisters crooned from the record player. The storm howled and rattled the door.

Ivy wrapped the blanket around the baby and glanced around the cozy room. "Joseph, will you pass out the gifts?"

Joe smiled and jumped to obey Ivy and reached underneath the Christmas tree. He walked around the room, handing out boxes and envelopes, and reached for the baby. "My turn, Miss Ivy."

Merry grinned as the big man scooped the tiny baby into his arms and jiggled the bundle as he walked around the room. A smile spread across his face, and he cooed at the baby.

Merry glanced away. Butterflies fluttered in her stomach at his sweet coos and gentle smiles. She'd always hoped to find a man who loved children, but Joe was her mother's friend.

Joe settled on the couch next to Merry and leaned over. "Look at her. She's so sweet." He reached out a finger to stroke the baby's finger. Merry's heart lurched at the grin on his face. He turned to her and smiled. "Do you want to hold her?"

Merry nodded and reached for the baby. Joe settled the bundle into Merry's arms, and their fingers brushed. Merry's eyes widened, and Joe winked. Her cheeks flushed, and she turned her head away from his gaze.

"Look at her," Joe whispered. "She's perfect."

Merry rubbed the baby's head and grinned. The little girl's mouth bowed into a tiny kiss, and she whiffled a snore. Merry giggled and glanced across the room at Angel. She sat in the recliner with her eyes closed.

"What names did you pick for her?" Merry asked.

Angel shrugged.

Merry frowned. *Why isn't she excited?*

Ivy stood and clapped her hands. "Let's get this party started. Joe, you first." Ivy pointed at the gift next to Joe. "Open it."

Joe struggled with the ribbon surrounding the box and pulled the red and green wrap off. He pulled a red wool scarf from the box and grinned. "Did you make this for me, Miss Ivy?"

Ivy smiled and nodded. She pointed to Merry. "Your turn." Her eyes sparkled in the light from the Christmas tree.

Joe held the box for Merry, and she opened the gift with her free hand. She pulled a delicate scarf from the package. Knit with fine yarn and edged in ruffles, the forest screen scarf represented hours of her mother's time. "Oh, Mom, it's gorgeous." Merry smiled, and her eyes stung. She blinked before the tear trickled down her cheek.

Joe reached for the scarf and wrapped it around Merry's neck. He gently smoothed the ruffles behind the baby in her arms. His eyes searched hers for a moment, and Merry glanced down. Heat rose in her cheeks, and she cleared her throat. "Your turn, Mom."

Ivy pulled the gingham paper from the box in her hands and gasped. "Oh, Merry." Tears ran down her cheeks, and she clutched a blanket. "How did you do this?"

Merry shrugged. "I found a lady online. Good thing I came for a visit because I forgot to mail it."

"Let me see," Joe said.

Ivy unfurled the blanket between her outstretched arms. A photo of Merry's father smiled from the fabric and handwriting embroidered across the bottom read, "I love you, Ivy girl."

"Dad's handwriting," Merry whispered to Joe.

He smiled. "A priceless gift, Miss Ivy."

Ivy hugged the blanket to her chest and sighed. "He called me Ivy girl from the first time he met me." A tear rolled down her cheek. "I miss him."

Merry swallowed over the lump in her throat and leaned down to kiss the baby's head.

"Anyone need a refill on coffee or rolls?" Joe glanced around the room.

"Coffee," Ivy said and held out a large Christmas mug. "Always coffee." She winked.

Joe disappeared into the kitchen, and Ivy sank onto the couch and planted a smooch on Merry's cheek. "Thank you, sweetheart."

Merry smiled. "Seeing his handwriting doesn't make you too sad?"

Ivy smiled. "No, it's precious."

Joe handed Ivy the mug and settled into the empty recliner next to Angel. He glanced at the new mother huddled under a brightly colored afghan and cleared his throat. “Angel, are you in trouble?”

Angel turned her head away from Joe and pulled the afghan around her shoulders. Ivy’s grandfather clock ticked, and a log snapped, sizzling in the woodstove. Bing crooned another Christmas classic, and Angel closed her eyes.

Merry patted the baby’s bottom and waited for someone to say something—anything.

“We want to help you,” Joe said and reached for Angel’s hand. She tucked her hand underneath the afghan.

Merry held her breath, and Ivy tapped her foot. Joe placed his fingers on his lips and shook his head.

“No one can help me,” Angel whispered. She stared at Merry and raised her chin. Her eyes blazed.

“Open your envelope,” Merry said.

Angel opened the envelope and stared at the card. Her hands trembled, and she dropped the card to cover her eyes. A tear trickled down her cheek, and she scrubbed it away.

Ivy grimaced and patted Merry's hand. Joe watched Angel.

When Angel finally glanced up, her face twisted into a scowl, and she stared at Merry and the baby. "No," she said.

"No, what?" Joe asked.

"No, I can't," Angel whispered. "This will never work."

"You can, and it will," Ivy said and smiled. "Let us explain."

Chapter Nineteen

Ivy grabbed a chair from the kitchen and sat near Angel. She reached out and patted the girl's knee. "How did you get here, Angel? Where are you from?"

Angel sobbed and reached for a tissue to dab her eyes.

Merry pulled the baby close to her chest as the weight of Angel's sadness settled over her. She took a deep breath and waited for Angel's response.

"We want to help you, Angel," Joe said. He sat on the floor in front of Angel's recliner. "Who are you running from?"

Angel glanced around the room and gripped the arm of the recliner. Her chin trembled when she whispered, "Her dad."

Joe nodded. "I figured as much, but how did you get here?"

"Where are you from?" Ivy asked.

Angel blew out a breath and wiped the sweat from her forehead. "I'm from Chicago."

Joe whistled. "How did you get here?"

Angel glanced around the room, and in a voice so low Merry had to lean forward to hear her, Angel told her story.

Merry's eyes glistened with tears when Angel finished. She patted the baby and whispered, "You poor thing."

Ivy sighed and stood with her hands on her hips. "Angel, nothing has changed. We meant what we said, and we're going to help you for as long as you need us."

"How will you do this? I don't know ..." She trailed off, and tears rolled down her cheeks.

"For starters, I lost my job before Christmas. I have nowhere to be and nothing to do. I'd love to be Auntie Merry to your baby girl." Merry leaned over and planted a kiss on the top of the baby's soft head.

"I'm a retired nurse and an empty nester." Ivy laughed. "Well, I was an empty nester until Merry came home. We have plenty of space and an empty bedroom too," Ivy said.

Joe stretched. "I'm around a lot too. I only work a few days a week as a paramedic. I do odd jobs the other days. I'm always willing to give Miss Ivy a hand."

Angel glanced around the room. She held onto the recliner arm with white knuckles, but her tears had slowed. She bit her lips and smiled a tiny smile.

"Angel, I know you want the best for your little girl, but she needs you more than anything. Stay here. Let us adopt you." Ivy smiled. "Not a real adoption, of course. But we will do everything in our power to support you so you can keep this precious baby safe and happy."

Angel's face crumpled, and she burst into heaving sobs.

Merry glanced at Ivy and frowned. Ivy placed her finger on her lips and shook her head. She reached out for the baby and eased her out of Merry's arms.

"Here's your baby, Angel." Ivy placed the sleeping bundle in the sobbing girl's arms.

Angel rocked back and forth and wailed, and tears pooled in Merry's eyes. The raw emotion Angel expressed tore at Merry's heart.

"Should we leave?" Merry whispered.

Ivy nodded, and Joe and Merry tiptoed to the kitchen.

"I cannot believe he kicked her out of the car in a blizzard and made her walk," Merry sputtered. She clenched her fists. "I'd like to give him a piece of my mind."

Joe poured coffee and set a steaming mug in front of Merry. "I don't understand men who treat women like that either, but God brought her to Ivy's door for a reason. I love your idea to adopt Angel and let her keep her baby instead of someone else adopting the baby."

Merry shrugged. “I don’t know why I had the idea, but she seemed so lost. I know someone would adopt the baby eventually, but what about Angel? Who would help her? She’s a baby herself.”

Joe nodded and sat across from Merry. “She’s had a hard life, but if anyone can help, it’s your mother.”

Merry smiled and chuckled. “Angel has no idea what she’s agreeing to.”

Joe grinned. “Your mother is a tough cookie, that’s for sure. But she has a lot of love to give too.”

“To you?” Merry asked. Her fingers traced circles on the tabletop, and she stared into the coffee mug.

“Me? What?” Joe stammered. “What in the world are you talking about, Merry?”

Merry glanced up and shrugged. “Well, you spend so much time here, and my mom lights up when you’re around. And you ...”

“No way, Merry. Your mom and I are friends. I help her out once in a while because her daughter deserted her.”

Merry's eyes blazed. "You are in no position to judge why I left Liberty Ridge. You have no idea."

Joe held up a hand. "All I know, Merry, is that your mother is alone running this big house and the land all by herself, and you're off living your best life in Atlanta."

Merry clenched her jaw and dropped her empty coffee mug on the table. "You are ridiculous." She marched outside, slamming the storm door.

Joe's voice carried out the door with her. "Ridiculous maybe, but at least I'm not a deserter."

Merry leaned against the back of the house and groaned. The blizzard hadn't slowed, and the wind howled. Snow pelted her with sharp icy points, and her breath swirled around her face in a steamy fog. She shivered and rolled her eyes. "Good one, Merry. Dramatically storm out into a blizzard without your coat."

She leaned against the back of the house until her goosebumps had goosebumps. When she turned to go inside,

Joe stood at the back door, grinning.

"What?" she snapped.

"You forgot your coat, didn't you? Now you have to come back inside and face me?" His deep chuckle almost caused Merry to forget why she had marched outside.

She glared and marched past him into the warm kitchen.

Ivy stepped into the kitchen and shivered. "Whoa. Who left the back door open?"

"Sorry, Miss Ivy, that was me," Joe said.

"Come back to the living room. Angel wants to share something, and I believe you'd like to hear her," Ivy said.

Merry and Joseph followed Ivy into the living room. Joe stopped to add another log to the woodstove and settled onto the couch next to Merry.

Ivy tucked a heavy afghan around Angel and the baby. Angel smiled up at Ivy and whispered, "Thank you." Her tears had stopped, but her red-rimmed eyes showed the crying sessions she'd had earlier.

Angel pulled the baby close to her chest and rubbed the tiny head. She leaned down and kissed the baby's head. Everyone laughed when a loud burp erupted from the little bundle. Angel glanced around the room and inhaled deeply.

"I always wanted her," she whispered. "I just didn't know what to do." She pulled the baby to her face and buried her nose in the baby's hair. Angel sobbed, and Ivy hurried to hold her hand.

Angel nodded her head and wiped her eyes. "My ... her father didn't want her, but I did. I had given up trying to keep her. He kicked me out of the car when I told him I wouldn't give her away. He pulled over and pushed me out. He didn't even let me grab my bags."

She sniffled, and Ivy patted her hand.

"When you caught me sneaking out, it wasn't that I didn't want to stay with her. I didn't know how I could, and you people seem so kind. I knew you'd love her and take care of her." She hid her face behind the baby and cried.

The lump in Merry's throat grew, and a tear trickled down her cheek. When Joe reached for her hand, she didn't pull away. She held his hand and choked back her tears as she watched a Christmas miracle unfold.

"I'm glad you were home," Angel smiled. "I don't think I had enough strength to keep walking if you hadn't opened the door."

Ivy patted her hand and smoothed the baby's dark hair. "I'm glad we were home too. And look how perfectly God worked everything out. A retired nurse, a paramedic, and my sweet daughter home for the holidays." She smiled at Angel. "God brought you to our door for a reason, and now it's your door too. I mean that with all my heart. We will help you raise this baby girl and help you get on your feet. But today, we're going to celebrate the birth of Jesus, and you're going to rest." She reached behind the chair to adjust the volume on the record player. Nat King Cole crooned out carols, and the lights twinkled behind Angel and the baby.

Merry kept her hand inside Joe's strong warm hand and leaned her head back onto the cushions to take in the scene. *Straight from a Norman Rockwell painting.* She sighed, and thankfulness flooded her soul. Her relationship with her mother had strengthened. She'd witnessed her first birth, and the thought of getting to know the man next to her made the long winter seem a little shorter.

Angel giggled and pointed at the couch.

Merry lifted her head. "What?"

"You two are Merry and Joseph, just like the Christmas story." Her eyes sparkled, and the smile that lit her face softened her features.

Merry's cheeks flushed, and she snatched her hand out of Joseph's. She pulled the afghan around her shoulders and frowned.

Joseph laughed and winked at Merry.

Ivy stood with her hands on her hips. "I'm about to put our Christmas dinner in the oven, but someone better name that little bundle pretty soon." She pointed at Angel and the baby.

A smile enveloped Angel's face, and she sighed. "I didn't choose a name for her because I didn't think I could keep her. But this morning, I knew. Her name is Hope."

Chapter Twenty

Epilogue

The Christmas lights twinkled, and Bing Crosby crooned Ivy's favorite carols from the record player. Logs crackled in the woodstove, and a cheerful warmth filled the cozy living room. Ivy hurried between the living room and kitchen, checking on the cinnamon rolls in the oven and the gift-wrapping party near the tree.

Angel laughed and pulled a ribbon from Hope's chubby fingers. "That's for Papa Joe's present, silly girl. Give it back."

Hope clutched the ribbon and cried around the pacifier in her mouth.

Merry laughed and swooped the baby into her arms. She patted the baby's dark curls and planted a kiss on her plump cheek. "I'm sorry your mama is so mean, sweetheart. Auntie Merry would let you play with the Christmas ribbons."

Angel sighed. "She's going to grow up spoiled rotten."

Merry shrugged. "Not my concern, Angel. It's your fault she's so precious. I can't help spoiling her. Don't know what to tell you."

Angel laughed, and her eyes sparkled. "When she's three and throwing fits in the store, she's your problem."

Merry kissed the baby's forehead and stared into her eyes. "You won't be a naughty three-year-old, will you, Hope? Be good, so your mama doesn't stop me from filling you with sugar and saying yes to everything you ask."

"Oh my." Angel laughed and pressed the final piece of tape on Joe's gift. "Do you think Joe will like this? It's only a Christmas tree made from Hope's handprints."

Merry nodded. "Joe loves everything you and Hope make for him. He'll most likely hang that over the fireplace." Merry tickled Hope. The baby giggled and laid her head on Merry's shoulder. Merry sighed and patted her back. "Someone's getting sleepy."

"I can't believe she's one today," Angel whispered.

"Hey, don't get all emotional now." Merry laughed. "Mother, Angel needs you," she called.

Ivy hurried into the living room, her nose smudged with flour. "What's wrong?" she demanded.

Angel shook her head. "Your daughter is just making fun of me for being sentimental about Hope turning one."

Ivy waved a wooden spoon at Merry. "Leave her alone. We mamas cry about our babies growing up." She kissed Merry on the cheek and patted Hope. "Joe said he'd come over after feeding his animals." She glanced at the clock. "Can you brew coffee, Merry?"

Merry handed Hope to Angel and followed Ivy to the kitchen. The spicy scent of cinnamon filled the warm room. "I'm glad I finally came home, Mom," she said.

Ivy patted her arm, leaving flour behind. "I'm glad you came home too, sweetheart."

"A year passed so quickly. I can hardly believe it. Do you think Hope will start walking soon?"

Ivy stirred milk into a bowl and shrugged. "Hard to say. Every baby develops at a different rate. You didn't take a step until you were sixteen months old. I thought you'd never walk." Ivy chuckled. "You let your daddy carry you everywhere."

Merry smiled even though the mention of her father brought a lump to her throat.

"Hard to believe nine years passed so quickly," Ivy whispered. She smiled at Merry and blew out a breath. "I miss him."

"Me too," Merry said. "But things feel brighter with Hope and Angel around, don't they?"

Ivy nodded. "Absolutely. I'm so glad because I didn't think I'd get grandchildren." She turned to Merry with a grin and snapped the dish towel toward her leg.

"Mom," she protested. "I'm not too old to have children."

"Well, the clock's ticking, and you don't seem to have any prospects." Ivy winked.

"I may have one or two lined up. You don't know everything about my life."

Ivy snorted. "Must have left him in Atlanta."

Merry laughed. "Oh, you're a funny one, Mother." Hope squealed, and Merry stepped into the living room. "Need anything, Angel?"

"Nope, just had to wrestle a bow from your niece once again." She rolled her eyes when Merry blew a kiss to Hope.

The door opened, and a blast of cold air followed Joe into the house. "Merry Christmas," he called and set down a pile of packages.

Merry shivered. "Brrr ... You're letting all our heat out."

"At least the sun is shining this year, and no blizzard." Joe smiled and pushed the front door closed. "Where's the birthday girl?"

Hope squealed and dropped to her hands and knees to crawl to Joe. He bent down to grab her and tossed the baby high.

Merry grimaced and glanced at Angel, who shrugged. "He hasn't dropped her ... yet."

The baby shrieked with laughter, and Joe tossed her again. "Papa Joe would never drop his sweet baby Hope, now would he?"

Ivy stepped into the room and rested her arm on Merry's shoulders. "Oh good, everyone's here. Let's settle in and open gifts before Hope needs her nap."

Merry glanced around the room. Her life had changed for the better. Her busy life in Atlanta was a hazy dream far in the past. The quiet pace of life in Liberty Ridge had always annoyed Merry, but now she relished each day. She worked at the realtor's office on Main Street and earned a ridiculously small paycheck. She spent most of the money on baby Hope and helped her mom with bills. She had a standing lunch date with Joe once a week, and they had moved past friendship, but while Merry was ready for more, she didn't know what Joe wanted. For now, spending time with him felt like a favorite sweater. She went to church with Ivy each Sunday and worshipped from her heart. The old high-powered Merry would have turned up her nose at the boring life the new Merry lived, but the new Merry enjoyed peace and happiness for the first time in years.

Hope ripped the paper off of her presents and chewed on the boxes. Angel scurried around the room, grabbing wrapping paper to keep Hope from eating the scattered pieces. Ivy clapped her hands and sang a song to the baby.

Merry turned to Joe, and her eyes widened. He knelt in front of her holding a small velvet box. "Joe?" Her voice rose into a high-pitched question. Ivy and Angel stood behind him, grins spread from ear to ear.

"Merry, I know we haven't known each other long, but I've enjoyed getting to know you over this past year. I've seen your tenderness with Hope and your love for your mom. I've seen you take Angel under your wing like a big sister, and I've seen you allow me to become part of this family. After realizing I wasn't here to steal your mama, that is."

Ivy laughed. Merry blushed and hid her face behind her hands.

"You are a beautiful treasure, and I'd be honored to spend the rest of my life with you." He opened the box, and a diamond ring sparkled in the light of the Christmas tree.

Angel gasped. "Goodness, Merry. You better say yes."

Joe winked. "Well, Merry?"

Merry swallowed the lump in her throat and blinked back happy tears. Hope pulled on her skirt, and Merry leaned down to grab the little girl. Hope settled onto Merry's lap and sucked her thumb. Merry sighed and looked into Joe's eyes. She nodded, and his eyes softened. A grin spread across his face as he slid the ring onto her finger.

She held out her hand and twisted it from side to side to catch the light of the Christmas tree. The ring sparkled and shimmered, and her heart beat with excitement for their future.

The baby stood on Merry's lap and pulled on Joe. He leaned in and kissed the baby's cheek at the same time that Merry kissed the other side. Their eyes met, and Merry sighed.

"You know what the best gift I've ever received for Christmas is?" she whispered.

"Yes." He tousled the baby's hair and squeezed Merry's hand. "Because it's the best gift I ever received for Christmas too. Hope."

A Letter From The Author

Dear Reader,

When I started writing Hope For Christmas, I planned to have Angel leave her baby with Ivy and Merry and disappear into the blizzard. But I wondered what would happen if the women and Joe supported Angel so she could mother her baby, and the story changed.

One person, one family cannot take care of every mother in need, but we can all do something.

If you want to support a woman like Angel, consider donating to your local pregnancy clinic. They always need help and are happy to extend volunteer opportunities to you.

What about "adopting" a local single mom and helping her? She might need help with errands or child care. Maybe she'd appreciate a gift card for gas or a favorite restaurant. Can you mow her lawn or watch her children so she can run errands or nap? What about helping with car repairs or home repairs? Include her in gatherings and invite her for coffee. Single moms need friends too!

We can't do everything, but we can do something. Put your thinking cap on and open up your heart to look for opportunities to bless a mom in need of support.

Thank you for reading my story and considering how you can support a mom today.

Malissa

Meet The Author

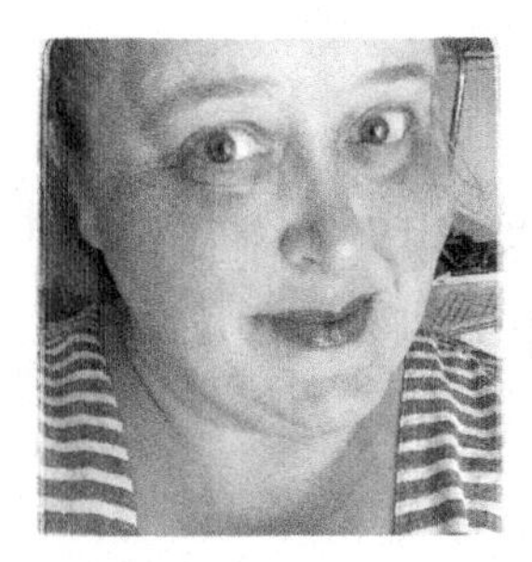

Malissa Chapin grew up reading books, making up stories, and vowing to publish a book before turning twelve. She's a few years late for her goal but still devours books and makes up stories.

Malissa loves creating with words, yarn, fabric, and watercolors. She enjoys sharing her faith, reading, collecting vintage treasures, drinking coffee, playing the piano, homeschooling her bonus baby, and looking on the bright side. She lives and sometimes freezes in Wisconsin with her family and a crazy cat.

Please visit my website (Just my name and add a dot com) and sign up for my newsletter. I'll update you on new releases and fun things about my writing journey.

Piper Haydn Murder Goes Solo August 2022

Piper Haydn is on the case when murder comes to peaceful Cranberry Harbor, Wisconsin. With her piano recital hours away, Piper's last need is a piano problem—or a murder problem! When her new piano arrives with the body of her ex-fiancé inside, suspicion rests on Piper.

To avoid a murder charge, she must shift her attention from music to murder. With a killer at large, Piper calls off the recital and closes the academy. Believing that she and her friends can solve the murder, Piper tries to clear her name and tries to discover what happened to her secretary Lisa. As the investigation crescendos, Piper leans on the support and creativity of her best friend Roosevelt and fellow music teacher Trefor to help solve the crime. Can Piper and friends solve the mystery before the killer solos in on another victim?

The Road Home

Sometimes your past catches up with you.

Sometimes you confront your past.

When a life of tragedy leaves Audra March with a desperate desire for acceptance, she blurs the line between right and wrong. She runs from her tainted past and creates a new identity in a small Wisconsin town. When she discovers a vintage recipe box, her search for the owner takes Audra across the country and sets her on a collision course with the truth. With the help of an Appalachian preacher and the long-buried deception of an elderly woman, Audra learns the value of honesty and trust. For the first time, she finds hope for her future. But when her carefully crafted identity is at risk, her resolve is tested. Will she run again? Or will she confront the consequences of her past? Can the truth set her free?

Made in the USA
Monee, IL
08 January 2024

51378819R00096